Lily Hyde is a British freelance writer and journalist based in Ukraine. She has been covering cultural and social issues in the former Soviet Union for several years, and her journalism and travel writing has been widely published in the international press. She has written short stories and is the author of *Riding Icarus*, her first novel for children.

Lily first learned about the Crimean Tatars when she wrote some news articles on Crimea, and found their history and the struggle for their homeland so inspiring she went on to write her second novel, *Dream Land*. She says, "I love listening to people's stories, trying to understand what they dream about, what makes them tick; wondering what our lives would be like if I'd been born in their place and they'd been born in mine. Everyone has an astonishing tale to tell, and the hardest thing about writing this book was that I just couldn't include them all."

Books by the same author

Riding Icarus

Dream Land

LILY HYDE

WALKER
BOOKS

First published 2008 by Walker Books Ltd
87 Vauxhall Walk, London SE11 5HJ

2 4 6 8 10 9 7 5 3 1

Text © 2008 Lily Hyde
Illustrations © 2008 Sarah Coleman

Extracts p21 and p22 from Edward A. Allworth
"My Tatarness, Shevki Bektore" in *The Tatars of Crimea*, p 77
© 1997 Duke University Press. All rights reserved.
Used by permission of the publisher.

The right of Lily Hyde to be identified as author of this work
has been asserted by her in accordance with the Copyright,
Designs and Patents Act 1988.

This book has been typeset in Cochin and Caslon Antique

Printed and bound in Great Britain by Clays Ltd, St Ives plc

British Library Cataloguing in Publication Data:
a catalogue record for this book
is available from the British Library

ISBN 978-1-4063-0765-8

www.walker.co.uk

For the Crimean Tatars

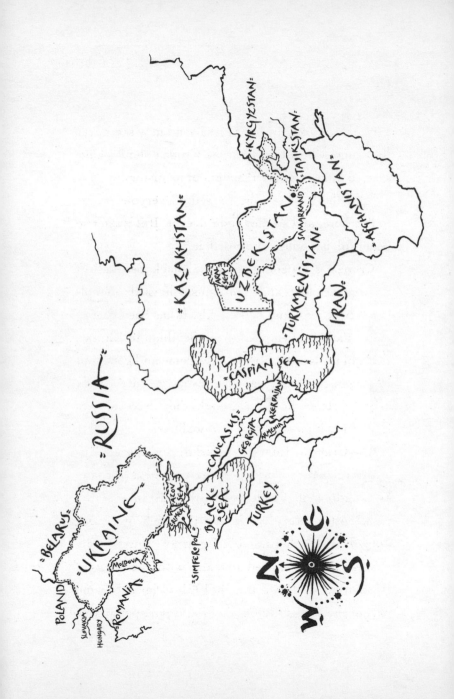

I once said to a Crimean Tatar friend how sad it was that such a beautiful place as Crimea should have seen so much warfare throughout its history.

"But that's why!" she replied. "Everyone wants to live here, and so they fight over it. If it wasn't so beautiful, it wouldn't be worth it."

Crimea is a peninsula in the Black Sea, full of flowery meadows and mountains, vineyards and villages, beaches – and battlefields. It has been part of many states and empires, from Scythian to Khazar, Mongol to Russian. Rulers have come and gone, but for seven hundred years the Crimean Tatars have called Crimea home, although they have always shared it with many other nationalities.

The Crimean Tatars are Muslim, and speak a language related to Turkish. They formed a khanate, or kingdom, in Crimea from the fifteenth to the eighteenth century, when the peninsula was conquered by Catherine the Great of Russia. The Russian empire ceased to exist with the Russian Revolution of 1917, and in 1921 Crimea became part of the Soviet Union. At first, Soviet policy was to support the different ethnic groups it incorporated, but that soon changed to repression. During the Second World War, the Soviet leader Joseph Stalin deported all the Crimean Tatars. They were resettled far away in Central Asia and Siberia, and prohibited from returning.

But the Crimean Tatars never ceased to call Crimea home. In 1986 a political process called perestroika began, which led eventually to the break-up of the Soviet Union into many independent countries. Under perestroika the laws were relaxed, and thousands of Crimean Tatars sold their houses, packed their bags and came home to Crimea.

L.H.

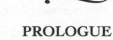

PROLOGUE

I'd tell them but I'm not sure they would understand. I thought I was going to die when we took off. I, who made this whole journey the other way among the thousands of us dying. Then, it took us eighteen days, south through the Caucasus, across the Caspian Sea, casting out the bodies from the cattle trucks at each stop. And now it's less than five hours: that's all the time it takes to bring us home. It's unnatural, this flying, but not inhuman. Inhuman is what they did to us fifty years ago.

I never thought I'd live to come back. Yet here I am with my daughter-in-law and grandchildren, and behind and in front other Crimean Tatars, row upon row of us, silent with hope and dread. Together we are remembering the horrors of our journey into exile: the wails, the prayers, the

9

shouts of the Russians as they cursed us for being traitors. Nearly fifty years gone, but I hear them still under the smooth humming of the aircraft pushing into my ears. The young flight attendant said it was the pressure, and brought round boiled sweets to suck. As if we were children to be comforted.

My grandson, Lutfi, was insulted and refused, ignoring the attendant's polished smile. He's thinking about his girl, the one he believes we don't know about. If I thought he'd listen I would tell him: leaving a girl behind in another land is not hardship, my fine young grandson. Taking your beloved with you into exile, and having her die in your arms: that's real suffering. Pray Allah you never live through that. Safinar, my Safinar, you'll never come home.

Next to me, my granddaughter squeals and squashes her nose to the small oblong of window. "The sea's finishing. I can see land! Is that it, Khartbaba? Is it?"

I take her hand, leaning across her to look. I love my granddaughter Safi the best, although I will never tell her so. Down below is too far away for my old eyes worn out by tears and the salt steppe. I can make out blue and green, and patches of white that my grandchildren assure me are clouds. If they had told me in the cattle trucks that I'd live to see clouds from the top downwards, it is I who would not have listened.

"Is it Crimea?" Safinar looks up at me, brimming with excitement.

I can't see but it doesn't matter. That green diamond set in the blue Black Sea, that almost-island we left behind almost fifty years ago – I know it as well as I know my Safi's face; all that time it has been engraved on my heart.

1

THE AIR OF YOUR HOMELAND
Crimea, Ukraine: 1992

At the bottom of the aeroplane steps, Safi thought she was not the only one wondering whether to kneel and kiss the ground. The passengers moved hesitantly, as if half expecting the firm earth to vanish, the way it does when you're just dropping off to sleep and suddenly, shockingly, you're falling. They had the look of people jerked awake – dazed, wondering, innocent. Grandpa bent and scraped up a few specks of gravel from the tarmac. "Home," he said doubtfully, shutting them in his big palm.

Home. It was what everyone was saying, the whole crowd off the plane from Uzbekistan, bundling bulging suitcases through the airport and into the shouting rabble of taxi drivers. Safi shrank behind Lutfi, but then there, miraculously, was Papa, bright-eyed and fiercer than ever, his face smudged with stubble and tiredness. He kissed Grandpa and Lutfi on the cheeks, hugged Mama, and at last his arm was round Safi, warm as she remembered. But then Papa seemed to be looking for someone else. Safi felt another pang of disbelief that Lenara wasn't with them; they'd had to leave her little sister behind in Uzbekistan because she was still too young to come back. Papa didn't know that Lenara stood nearly as tall as Safi's chest now, that she could write her name, and she had a big gap where her front teeth had come out and the new ones hadn't grown yet.

For the last six months, Papa had been away from his family, sorting out their new home here in Crimea. Their *true* home, Safi corrected herself. Crimea seemed new and unknown, but really it wasn't at all; it was the place where, as long as she could remember, she'd been told she belonged.

Oh, but it felt strange. Squashed up on Mama's knee in the back of the car, she gazed, subdued, at the grey town of Simferopol, full of strangers in dark coats. Papa's old friend Mehmed was driving;

he'd given Safi a kiss tickly with moustache, and at every red traffic light he turned round to smile at them. Lutfi was looking out of the window too, watching the girls passing by. When Safi caught his eye she gave him a secret sympathetic smile. That was another thing Papa didn't know: nobody except Safi knew that her brother was in love.

As the town gradually gave way to countryside, Mehmed slowed the car and pointed to a muddy brown field rising to low hills. "Look."

The slope was covered in orderly rows of tents and tarpaulin shelters, barely distinguishable from the grass and mud. Between the tents, lines of shirts and trousers and the occasional striped silk dress hanging out to dry made splashes of colour.

"It looks like an army camp," Lutfi said. "Except for the dresses."

A fine bluish haze of woodsmoke covered the camp, and its smell, mixed with that of roasting mutton and rice, reached them as they drove slowly past.

"It's us, the Crimean Tatars," Papa said. "It's a camp now but it will be a town, one day soon. Whether we get permission or not, we'll build it."

They left the camp behind and drove on past

orchards of low, leafless trees. The hills on the darkening horizon started to heave themselves into abrupt cliffs and plateaux, snow still lying pale in the folds of them. Grandpa gazed and gazed, until suddenly he said imperiously, "Stop the car."

They opened the doors and the early March air flooded in: fresh, quiet, with an edge of damp chill. Grandpa unfolded himself from his seat and stood on the grassy roadside, breathing deeply.

"I know these trees." There was still a touch of doubt in his voice. He said, more confidently, "I know those hills. I know this air."

Wanting to stretch her legs, Safi climbed out after him. She watched as her grandfather knelt stiffly and did what she'd thought about at the airport: he actually bowed and kissed the earth. When he stood up again, he had tears in his eyes. Mama and Papa and Lutfi had joined them on the roadside, and suddenly – Safi didn't know how it happened or quite why – they were all hugging and talking and crying and laughing.

From the car Mehmed watched indulgently before starting up the engine again. "Yes, it's good to be where we belong," he called, "but we have much to do to claim it back."

As if something in the air had made them slightly drunk, the rest of the journey they all talked like crazy.

"What do you mean, claim it back?"

"When will it be a town?"

"Is it the same as you remember, Ismail *Aga*?" Mehmed asked Grandpa.

"The hills don't change. The soil. But where are the peach trees? And the villages…"

"How does it feel, children, the air of your homeland?"

"It feels like growing things. Different than in Samarkand," Lutfi reflected. "You can tell it rains more."

"Asim, what about the permission? Have we got it yet?"

"It doesn't matter. We will."

"But, Asim, the children. You promised me."

Papa patted Mama's knee. "I couldn't do it any longer without you. I wanted to bring you home. I want you all to take part in this. You hear me, children?" He looked at Lutfi and Safi. "We lost this land of ours nearly fifty years ago. And now we're claiming it back. I want you to see it and know it and claim it yourselves."

"You bet," Lutfi said flippantly. But it was the wrong answer for Papa's fierce excitement and he added quickly, "I know. I do know. And I … I'll do my best."

"And you, Safinar?"

Safi looked away from those unknown, cold hills outside. She whispered, "Yes."

Papa laughed and put his hands on each side of her head, tucking his fingers between her careful plaits. "That's my girl. Oh, how I've missed my family! And now tell me about my other little girl. How tall is Lenara? How many teeth has she got?"

It was dark when they arrived at Bakhchisaray, so Safi could see little of the old capital of the Crimean Tatars where long ago Grandpa had gone to school. She looked out eagerly for the mosques and the khan's palace, but all she saw was ordinary houses with warmly lit windows.

Mehmed turned off the road and they began a bumpy ascent up a dirt track. The same smell of smoke and cooking reached them, and the head-lights picked out low humped shapes rather like haystacks.

"Army camp number two," said Mehmed cheerfully, braking. He switched off the headlights and everything outside turned black, sprinkled with dots of dim yellow light.

"Another town in the making," Papa said. "Out you get."

"Is this where you've been living for the last six months, Papa?" No mosque, no palace. As Safi's eyes got used to the darkness she could make out rows and rows of tents and shelters made of plastic sheeting draped over sticks and planks. The points of light came from paraffin lamps, and campfires glowed. A radio muttered away quietly to itself, and somewhere someone was singing an old Tatar song.

Papa took her hand, leading her down a line of shelters. "Most of the time I was camping outside the town hall, which was *much* more uncomfortable than here."

"Why outside the town hall?"

"Because we were picketing, to demand that the authorities give us back our land by Mangup-Kalye, where your grandfather grew up. That land belongs to our family; it always has. You know that, don't you, Safi?"

18

Of course Safi did. She'd known it for as long as she'd known anything. She was a Crimean Tatar, and her people had lived in Crimea for centuries, until the Second World War when the Soviet government had deported all the Crimean Tatars and let more Russians and Ukrainians settle in their place. Safi's parents, Lutfi and she and Lenara had all been born and had grown up in Uzbekistan. But that didn't change anything. Crimea was her home and now, since perestroika, she and all the other Tatars could finally return to it.

"But if it belongs to us, why do the authorities have to give it back?" she asked Papa.

"Exactly. And since they don't want to, we've decided to take it for ourselves. Soon you'll see the house we're building there, in Grandpa's village. But for the moment we're going to stay here in Bakhchisaray. Do you like it?"

"It's exciting." Safi had felt sleepy in the car, but now the smoke and darkness and the twinkling lamps made her feel wide awake and fluttery with half-scared delight. Some of the shelters glowed from inside like great dim lanterns, and shadows slid enormously over the walls. People called out from the entrances, or stopped to shake Papa's hand

19

as they walked past, and they touched Safi's head and patted her shoulders with quick warm touches, as if she were a kind of talisman.

"*Salaam aleikhum!*"

"It's good to see children."

"Another young one to join the fight."

"To reclaim the homeland…"

"Welcome home!"

Safi ducked her head, not entirely liking the many hands muzzing the plaits Mama had tied for her all that way away in Samarkand, in another country now. She was glad when they reached their tents, piled high inside with quilts and blankets. They all squashed into one, for company, and Mehmed brought them green tea and bowls of hot rice *plov*.

Papa sat with his arms round Mama. "I see you haven't been pining away for me, Elmira. Look at you; you've got fat."

"It's all the extra clothes!" Mama protested. "And a few lovely pieces of paper hidden you-know-where."

Tucked inside her bra and tights Mama was carrying money, everything that was left from the sale of their house after they had bought the air tickets.

Safi knew it wasn't as much money as Mama had hoped; in the last months since the Soviet Union had collapsed, everything – even houses – had lost value.

"Oh well, in that case…" Papa murmured something into Mama's ear, and she pushed him away with one of those sweetly indignant giggles Safi hadn't heard since her father had left.

Grandpa took out his pipe and thumbed tobacco into the bowl. The paraffin lamp fizzed peacefully. Outside, the voice was still singing. Safi didn't speak much Tatar – she spoke Russian like everyone else – but she knew the words to this song. For the last fifty years it had been forbidden because it spoke of their exile, but almost every Tatar child she knew had been taught the words secretly.

> *"Wherever I went, I found the scattered Tatars*
> *Without a single flowering rose to smell*
>
> *True wanderers in their own homes and gardens*
> *But these are secrets; who can you really tell?"*

It was a sad song, but the man's voice didn't sound

sad at all, because there was no one now to forbid him to sing it.

"The wind has tossed them to the rocks and mountains
This imperfect world has become a grave for the Tatars..."

Images from the long, long day began to flick through Safi's head. The sea spread out like a dull blue carpet far below the aeroplane, turning jade green around the crinkly Crimean coastline. She'd never seen the sea before. But she couldn't hold it; the waves were flowing backwards, turning into the sway and jerk of the bus they'd taken to the airport; and then she was back before that in Samarkand, in their empty, strangely echoing house. The boxes and bags were piled up in the doorway and the rooms where she'd lived all her life looked huge, emptied of all their furniture and pictures and people: nothing to fill them now but dusty sunlight. As she turned to go into her bedroom for one last time, the floor suddenly gave way and she was falling.

She jumped violently. For a second she was nowhere, and then she was wide awake again and she was somewhere. She was in a tent in Crimea, and her home in Samarkand was far, far away. It would always be far away now, because this strange new place Crimea was home.

"*Khartbaba*, will you tell me a story?" She was addressing Grandpa, but when her voice came out plaintive as a little girl's she looked slightly apprehensively at her father. She had turned twelve while he had been away; perhaps he would think she was too old now for bedtime stories.

Papa only smiled and nodded, nuzzling Mama's hair. Even Lutfi, who was quite grown up at fifteen, propped himself up on one elbow expectantly.

Grandpa's pipe smoke twirled out of the tent doorway. There was a rising moon over the camp now, turning the cloud edges to silver. "All right then…"

Safi wondered if he knew that she wanted a story to fill the cold space inside her and make her feel homey as his stories always did, because he'd been telling them to her for as long as she could remember. She smiled at him, a smile that felt a bit wobbly. Of course he knew. Grandpa knew everything.

2

DID YOU THINK WE WOULDN'T COME BACK TO HAUNT YOU?

"I know what it's like to arrive at a camp full of homeless people in a strange place, because that's what happened to me during the war," Grandpa said. "To all of the Crimean Tatars, when the Soviets forced us into exile in 1944. The trains took us to many places in Central Asia and Siberia. Mine went to Uzbekistan, to the Hungry Steppe."

Lutfi chased the last few rice grains around his bowl of *plov*. "It was called that because nothing grew there, right?"

"Nothing but thorns. The boggy ground was mixed with coarse white salt that blew away in the wind, so there was always a taste of it on your lips and a feel of grit in your eyes. It was a kind of cruel joke because the constant flavour of salt was like the ghost of food, but there was nothing to eat. All we got was sweetcorn: cornbread, corn porridge, even just dry kernels to chew. Sometimes not even that. It was the hungriest place in the world.

"The Soviet soldiers who came to take us away told us we were accused of collaborating with the Germans, and this was our punishment. But they would not say where we were going, and they gave us just fifteen minutes to get ready. So I had three shirts on my back, two pairs of trousers and my good boots, and in my pack I had a couple of books, a few roubles, and wrapped in my scarf and waistcoat our family coffee pot and coffee grinder."

"That's all?" Safi thought about all her nice things in Samarkand, boxed up ready to come to Crimea.

"That's all. The roubles had already gone by the time we arrived at the Hungry Steppe, and my boots soon followed, exchanged for bread. You see, I'd rather go barefoot than sell our coffee pot and grinder, even though I thought I'd probably never set eyes on a coffee bean again. But in the end the pot and the grinder had to go; I sold them to a brutal pig of a soldier who was a tea drinker, like all Russians, but he wasn't very bright and he liked the shiny brass.

25

"After that, even if I'd had something left to sell, no one would buy because there was no food at all. Even the guards were on reduced rations. There was a village a few kilometres away where we were sure there would be food. But we couldn't take one step outside the camp without permission. If we did we would be beaten and locked up – if they didn't simply shoot us first."

Safi tried to imagine Grandpa as a boy, just a year or two older than Lutfi, starving in the Uzbek steppe. Uzbekistan was where she had been born, and she'd loved living there. But when Grandpa had arrived nearly fifty years ago it had been an alien, hostile place of cold and deprivation.

"But at least being shot is quicker than dying of hunger," Grandpa went on, and Lutfi laughed and said, "That's what I'd think too."

"So I decided to try and get to this village to beg or steal some food. I slipped out in the dark, cleared the camp fence and set off without being seen. But I had forgotten one thing."

"What?"

Grandpa looked out again at the sky, but now the clouds hid any brightness. "The moon. It was huge and round and white, shining on the white acres of salt.

Ah, never have I seen such a moon since! I saw moon mirages. The salt stood up in fabulous dead palaces; it lay in shimmering lakes. And there was I, like a mouse on a lamplit tabletop, with nowhere to hide.

"And then I heard footsteps and humming, and from the camp came the stupid young soldier, the one who had taken our coffee pot and grinder in return for a miserable spoonful of corn porridge. He was strolling over the salt steppe and, Allah bless us, he had the pot and grinder in his hands and was admiring how they shone in the moonlight. I told you he was a bit touched. You could almost have felt sorry for him, had he not treated us so badly...

"I didn't dare move. I stood there, frozen, as he polished the coffee grinder on his sleeve and began to turn the handle.

"And the air filled with the most delicious smell of coffee. I couldn't believe it. I suppose it was the coffee dust still left in there after years of grinding, which all the long journey and the dirt and the salt had not managed to dislodge. But it felt like a dream. It was as if my poor senses, deranged by hunger and the moon, had conjured up this aroma like a mirage to torture me. And before I could help it I let out a deep groan."

Grandpa groaned, so deeply that Safi jumped.

"At once the soldier dropped the grinder, grabbed his pistol and shouted, 'Stop! You aren't allowed to leave the camp! Who are you? Speak!'

"But I couldn't. It was the wonderful smell of coffee, which took me straight home to my father's house. All I could do was make another deep and horrible groan.

"The soldier's hand with the pistol began to tremble. 'Who are you? I'll shoot!'

"I was struck with a sudden amazing idea. We Crimean Tatars spent all day breaking up and draining that salty plain, ready for a cotton plantation. Our clothes, our faces and hands were completely covered with salt dust, and in that fantastic moonlight I must have glowed white as a ghost. I lifted my arms and groaned a third time as hideously as I could, and intoned, 'Did you think I wouldn't come back to haunt you?'

"'H-haunt me?'

"'Yes, you! Look at your hands. Look at the blood on them!'

"The soldier screamed, 'Go away! Who are you? Where did you come from?'

"'You know who I am,' I said sepulchrally. 'And I

came from … there!' I pointed at the coffee grinder. 'I am the ghost who will never let you go. We Crimean Tatars never give up, not even if you kill us!'

"Oh, how that soldier cried. Like a baby. 'Leave me alone, God help me!' And he ran away from me as fast as he could.

"'We *never* give up!' I shouted after him. Then I couldn't shout any more for laughing. That moon, it went straight to my head. I picked up the coffee pot and grinder, went back to the camp, got over the fence and under my blanket, and slept like the dead until next morning."

Lutfi was laughing too. "What happened to the soldier?"

"He never came back." Grandpa tapped out the ash from his pipe and returned it to its little pouch. "The next day, a shipment of corn arrived."

"So you didn't starve after all." Safi was glad. It was a funny story, but sad too. "But, *Kharthaba*, who were you the ghost of?"

Grandpa sighed. "Oh, Safi. There were so many ghosts to choose from, in those terrible days. Too many."

"Isn't that what we've come home for?" Papa said suddenly. "To lay them to rest."

3

GHOSTS

A path led from the high, stony field where the Tatars were going to build their houses, down into Bakhchisaray. From up here the town was a jumble of rooftops, spiked with two tall mosque minarets beside the khan's palace. Safi waited at the top of the path, watching the short, upright figure of her grandfather toil up it towards her, and hopping with impatience. She was longing to hear about his visit to the town. Years ago, when he was a boy, he had walked there every day to lessons in the old Zindjirli *medresse*, and then to the fountain where the boys and girls loitered away each long, rose-scented sunny afternoon. It was always sunny in Grandpa's stories about Crimea.

Safi's smile as Grandpa reached her was a little puzzled, a little disappointed. She held the umbrella up to cover his head in its round black sheepskin *kalpak*, and asked, "*Khartbaba*, did it often rain like this when you lived here?"

"Real Crimean mud," Grandpa replied, lifting a shoe ponderous as a moon boot with clagging soil.

The rain had hardly stopped since they'd arrived two days ago. It was a fine, gauzy rain such as Safi had never seen before, and she might have enjoyed it had they not been living in a tent. Water ran in rivulets down the canvas and pooled around the tent pegs. The walls sagged and ballooned inwards with damp. The ground, churned up by digging and building work, turned to thick clayey mud that was impossible to clean off their clothes. The campfires spat and smoked sulkily; even the bread was soggy. It was miserable. Safi was looking forward to hearing about Grandpa's morning to remind her of all the stories she loved and cheer herself up.

"Did you go to the khan's palace? What about the fountain?"

"All the fountains have gone. Every single one." Grandpa took the umbrella and held it over them both, tucking Safi's hand into its accustomed place

31

under his arm. "And the khan's palace is a museum, but it was all closed up. I felt like a ghost. You remember the smell of coffee in the Hungry Steppe?"

"Of course. From our coffee grinder."

"That smell was real; it took me home. And now that I really am home in Crimea…" He couldn't carry on.

"What, *Khartbaba*?" Safi prompted. "Did you smell coffee in Bakhchisaray, from the cafes?"

"All the cafes have gone too. The smells, even the sounds have changed. Before, in the mornings, you'd hear the clatter of apprentices taking down the shutters from the workshops, calling to the customers. The mornings were busy, but the afternoons were slow and lazy and full of the click of backgammon pieces from the coffee houses. And Tatar spoken everywhere. Now there's only Russian, Russian, Russian. In those days, of course we knew Russian too but everyone in Crimea spoke Tatar – Greeks, Armenians, Russians, Karaims, it didn't matter. Now no one remembers our language."

He didn't mean to sound accusing, but Safi hung her head. She'd gone to classes with Lutfi, but Tatar had seemed hard to learn and, to be honest, a bit pointless in Uzbekistan, where nearly everyone spoke Russian.

Grandpa was still far away in his memories. Bakhchisaray had changed so much, he could almost doubt that the clean, lively town he remembered had ever existed. It was as if he had dreamt the whole place.

"And what about the *medresse*?"

Grandpa looked down at her. "You tell me about the Zindjirli *medresse*, Safi."

He had told her a hundred stories about it. Grandpa's father's brothers, and *their* fathers and brothers, had studied there; it was the oldest Muslim Tatar school in Crimea. "It was built by Khan Mengli Giray," she said promptly. "And he hung three chains over the doorway, so the students had to bow their heads when they went in."

"That's right. Three chains hung long ago to suspend the Zindjirli *medresse* like a golden box from paradise. Those chains are still there, and still you must bow your head, but the people passing under them are like ghosts."

"What do you mean?" Safi's eyes were round.

"It has a high wall around it now, with a padlocked gate and a guardhouse."

"And what's inside?"

"Inside, when I looked through the gate, I saw such people…"

Despite the rainy weather, there had been several men and women wandering in the *medresse* grounds. Most of them wore very shabby clothes, or even pyjamas. It was hard to tell what they were doing. They had an abstracted air of trying to remember something, as if they'd been sent on an errand but forgotten what it was halfway through, and now weren't quite sure where they were or why.

"I couldn't understand it," Grandpa told Safi. "Who were they? It was like something from a nightmare, when a place you know and love is suddenly full of strangers: no, not just strangers but creatures who have lost their souls. There was something inexplicably *wrong* about these people wandering around so aimlessly. As I watched, a woman in a white coat came round the corner of the building and started shooing them inside like chickens. And then the guard noticed me."

The guard had shouted at Grandpa, "Hey! How did you get out?"

"Out from where?" Grandpa was bewildered.

The man approached slowly, speaking in an

overloud voice, as if to someone very stupid or very old. "Come along now. Back you go." He took hold of Grandpa's sleeve.

"Let go of me," Grandpa said severely. "What have you done to the Zindjirli *medresse*?"

"Don't you worry about no zindjermy dresser. Let's get you in where you belong." The guard shouted over his shoulder at the white-coated woman, "Got one of your patients here. Reckon he must've got out somehow."

The woman hurried over to stare through the bars of the gate. She saw Grandpa's round sheepskin cap and snapped, "Don't be ridiculous. He's a Tatar. This used to be an old Tatar school or something."

"A Tatar? You sure?"

"Of course I'm sure. Honestly, these people!" the woman huffed. "They come here and expect us to give everything back to them, like the last fifty years never happened."

The guard let go of Grandpa's arm with a disgusted look. "Psychos, Tatars, what's the difference? All right, beat it, old man. Or we'll lock you up in here after all – don't think we won't. Best place for people like you."

Grandpa was angry, but he turned away. There was no point in arguing.

"After that, I just wanted to get back to my family and my people," he told Safi, winding up the story. "I felt like I'd had enough of Bakhchisaray for one day."

Safi was frowning. "I don't get it. The guard thought you were a patient from a hospital?"

"Not just any hospital. The *medresse* has been turned into a psychiatric ward. He thought I was an escaped lunatic."

"*No!*" Safi didn't know whether to laugh or be outraged, and came out with a snort that was a bit of both. "That's crazy! You don't look like a lunatic!"

The snort made Grandpa smile. "Those poor mad people. Maybe it wasn't such a silly mistake. They looked as lost as I feel here, now that everything's gone."

"You're not lost," Safi said indignantly. She tucked her hand tighter under her grandfather's arm, leaning close. "And it can't all really be gone. We're going to your village tomorrow, Adym-Chokrak. Then you'll see."

"Oh, my Safinar." Grandpa wasn't sure if it was

Safi leaning closer to him, or him leaning closer to her. Bakhchisaray had made him feel so tired and old. If I thought you'd understand I'd tell you, he thought. I am like those patients in the *medresse*, no longer knowing where they are or why. Your hand under my arm feels like the only thing anchoring me here.

"Let's go this way." Safi steered Grandpa quickly towards the Tatar camp, away from the group of children from Bakhchisaray who were loitering at the edge of the field, staring and pointing and shouting.

"What are they saying?" Grandpa asked, straining to hear.

"Oh, nothing." Safi tried not to sound upset. She was painfully missing her friends back in Samarkand. Most of the Tatars in the camp were men or boys of Lutfi's age or older, who had come back to Crimea ahead of their families. Lutfi was always off talking with them, but there was hardly anyone of Safi's age, so at first she'd been pleased to see the local children.

The locals, though, didn't want to make friends.

"Go home… Dirty Tatars…" Their shouts pursued them towards the shelters. At least no one threw any mud this time.

"They don't sound very welcoming," Grandpa observed.

"They're not." Safi was almost too hurt to feel properly angry. In Uzbekistan she'd had lots of Russian friends; she couldn't remember ever being picked on because of her nationality. "They're saying stupid things about us being Tatars."

And that was the real change, Grandpa thought. Not the vanished fountains and mosques but these local people, the Soviet Russians and Ukrainians who had locked up their mentally ill in the *medresse* and let Bakhchisaray crumble into grey rubbish-filled shabbiness.

"Years ago, we all lived here together," he said. "Russian, Tatar, Ukrainian. And then in the war the Soviet authorities decided we had sided with the German fascists, and they exiled us. Some Russians never liked us Tatars much, but it was the Soviets who taught them to hate us. They've hated us ever since."

Grandpa paused to negotiate a big puddle. "When the Soviet soldiers took us away in 1944, they couldn't have known what they were doing," he went on slowly, more to himself than to Safi. "They said we had betrayed them, but it was them that betrayed Crimea. By deporting us Tatars, they cut out its soul. All those years in exile, we kept ourselves alive by tending the soul of Crimea. But for all our care, I don't know whether in the end it turned into a ghost. Just a ghost."

4

WHERE IS OUR VILLAGE?

Safi scrambled from the car, staring in disbelief. Bedraggled ducks floated on an opaque pea-green pond. A dirt road led up the narrow valley, past two tents and a half-ruined building of spongy-looking yellow blocks. The woods cloaking the mountainous slopes of Mangup-Kalye closed them in with silence and with noise. The noise was the racketing birds, and the silence was what they couldn't fill with their singing: a huge, echoing void. Birdsong and silence that had not known people for a long, long time.

"Where is it? Where's Adym-Chokrak? Where is our village?"

Safi sat down on the grass with a bump, she was

so disappointed. Even after the shock of the camp in Bakhchisaray, she'd still thought the village would be exactly as Grandpa had described it. She knew it off by heart, although she'd never been there. The two-storey house where Uncle Murat and Aunt Halide lived, the *chaykhana* under the walnut tree, and the headman Ali Memetov's place smothered in grapevines, where they made wine even though the Koran said they weren't allowed to drink it. The fat-tailed sheep, the cobbled alleys that led to the fountain, the tobacco leaves laid out to dry in the sunshine.

All of it had gone. Every last scrap and stone.

Behind her, there was a splosh and an indignant quacking from the ducks; Lutfi had heaved a lump of mud into the soupy pond and was staring at the widening ripples. Papa squeezed Mama's hand where they stood by the car. And Grandpa blinked at the empty echoing valley and said, "Well, we've got some rebuilding to do."

Mehmed and Papa had already made a start. The yellow block building was half finished, not half ruined, and it was the house where Safi's family was going to live.

It was small and square, built of blocks of crushed shell that looked crumbly as sugar, but when Safi touched them they were hard and sharp-edged. Most of the house so far was underground: a cellar for their container of belongings when it arrived from Uzbekistan. Over it, raw splintery planks had been laid to make a floor. The walls stood just a little taller than Safi. A single small window was finished but it had no glass, just thin boards. A sheet of plastic was stretched over the top of the walls. When Safi peered inside, it was darkly poky and smelt of damp cement; three forlorn iron bedsteads, a dusty stool, a jumble of tin cups and plates.

"This is our house?" There could only be three rooms in there. No bathroom, no bedrooms.

The mixture of rage and disappointment must have shown in her face, because Grandpa said in his slow deep voice, "When we arrived in the Hungry Steppe we lived in dugouts. In holes in the ground. That was all that was waiting for us, Safinar."

"Yes, I *know*! You've told us a million times." Safi was shocked. She clapped her hand over her mouth and looked round to see if anyone else had heard how disrespectful she had just been. She'd never talked to her grandfather in that tone before. She wasn't sure she'd ever even *wanted* to. But something about the sight of the gloomy rubbishy half-built hovel made her stomach twist. She knew Grandpa had lived in a dugout. She knew the Tatars had been forced to build their own work camps in exile. She knew they'd had malaria and lice and only the clothes they stood up in. But she couldn't care about that, when all she could think of was *her* house, the one they'd left behind to come here.

"And I've told you a thousand times about this village we had to leave in Crimea," Grandpa said sternly. "It's gone now, but it's still in our blood, our bones."

Safi turned away so that he wouldn't see how angry she was. She had lived in a proper house in Samarkand, with six rooms and a veranda. The sun shone in warm squares through the clean curtains; the coffee pot and cups gleamed on the shelf. In her neat cosy bedroom the fringe on her lampshade danced as Lenara jumped up at it; at about five o'clock its shadow touched the door lintel like a reaching hand. And there was her friend Jemile climbing over the back fence and tapping on the window, coming to play.

Grandpa hadn't left behind his best friend. He hadn't left behind his little sister. It was all right for him to talk about blood and bones and building.

Safi left her family clustered about the little shack

and wandered away up the valley. It was a soft grey afternoon, but the steep leafless woods blocked out much of the light. When she went on along the road, she could see up the slopes to where ridges of rock appeared – one, two, three, four – right at the top of Mangup-Kalye like the spines of a great dragon. She didn't think she wanted to live in their shade. It was so utterly different from what Grandpa had told her. She didn't see how it could all have disappeared so completely, the red and white houses and the tobacco field, the fountain and the grapevines. There was not a single thing here she could recognize. Nothing in Crimea was like Grandpa had said.

A stone slipped under her foot, and the grating noise was so loud she stopped in fright. Without noticing, she must have turned a corner. Her family and the house and pond were out of sight. The dirt road led on in front of her, and the high silent slopes of wood and rock towered on either side, shutting her in. In the furthest outcrop of rock there was a window of light, like an eye looking down the valley, watching her.

Safi was so scared she couldn't breathe. She couldn't move. The eye pinned her. There was an eye in the rock.

"Safi!" Her mother's voice, a little anxious, wonderfully normal, floated up the valley. "Safinar! Where are you?"

"Hey, Safi!" Lutfi's voice was nearer, and a moment later he came round the bend in the track. "What are you doing, all on your own? Looking for Grandpa's house? I think we've found it, but there's nothing to see. Just a few old fruit trees." Lutfi sounded fed up. "I hope we don't really come and live here; it's dismal. Mehmed says there are still caves at the top of the mountain, and ruins and stuff. Sounds like there's more left up there than down here. What's the betting we end up living in a cave…"

Just before they turned the bend in the track, Safi dared to look back. The eye in the outcrop of rock had disappeared.

That night in the camp at Bakhchisaray, Mama and Papa argued. Safi lay in the tent she shared with Lutfi and Grandpa and listened to their heated undertones while Grandpa snored gently.

"But the land isn't ours," Mama said. "It's illegal; we'll be squatters with no rights and the authorities can come and turn us off it whenever they like."

"It was our fathers' land before the Soviets evicted them illegally. We've got the right of history."

"Since when have governments taken any notice of history?" Mama asked. "Yes, there's no Soviet Union any more, but Crimea's part of Ukraine now, and there's no Ukrainian law that says we can have the land."

"Then we'll make them write a law."

Mama changed tack. "How will we live in Adym-Chokrak? It's the middle of nowhere. There's nothing left. I want to work, Asim. I want Safi and Lutfi to go to school. Lutfi'll be thinking about college soon, and jobs. I don't want to risk everything on this dream of your father's."

"You shouldn't talk like that," Papa said sharply.

"I mean no disrespect. I wanted to come home to Crimea too, you know that. But here in Bakhchisaray at least we'll have friends and neighbours, our people, our culture. We'll have support; we can make a life. Out there, under that terrible mountain, that Mangup-Kalye..."

"I've been talking to Mehmed. He thinks that 'terrible mountain' is our opportunity. The ruins on Mangup are famous; there's a whole ancient city up at the top. There'll be tourists in the summer and we can start a business: guides, a campsite, a cafe. And it's not far from Bakhchisaray, so the children will be able to go to school."

"And me? What about my job?"

There was a silence.

"You shouldn't be thinking of your job now. There are more important things. We aren't in the godless Soviet Union any more; here we're going to be a proper Muslim Tatar family, live like our fathers did. That's why we came back."

Another silence, which went on this time.

"Safi, are you awake?" Lutfi hissed. She could just see him sitting up in the darkness by the entrance to the tent.

"Yes."

"Come over here."

Safi wondered if he'd been listening to their parents too. She couldn't remember the last time she'd heard them argue. She shuffled out from under her quilt and over to his side, careful not to disturb their grandfather.

Lutfi had opened the entrance and was looking out. Down at the bottom of the hill, between the outlines of the shelters, campfires glowed and black figures passed to and fro, sticks in their hands.

"They're looking out for the locals, in case they attack us," Lutfi whispered. "I heard Papa and Mehmed talking about it. They hate us here. They want us to go back to Uzbekistan."

"All because of a war fifty years ago." Safi shivered miserably. "I wish they would like us."

"I don't. It's not just because of the war. It's because they're occupying our land and they know they've got no right to it, and they don't want to give it back. That's what everyone says, here in the camp." Lutfi's eyes gleamed a little in the firelight and he shifted with unfamiliar impatience.

"I just want Lenara to come and for us to be a family again," Safi said dolefully. Suddenly, big girl that she was, she felt as if she was going to cry. Mama and Papa, even Lutfi now, felt distant and different, talking about strange things, and she missed her little sister.

"Oh, silly old Safi." But Lutfi was still the same person really. He put his arm round her, hugging her tightly, and a faraway, mournful tone crept into his voice so she knew he was thinking about his girl-friend back in Samarkand. "Everything'll be all right. And if it isn't, maybe we'll go home again."

5

CRIMEAN TATAR STAR ALLEY

Three days later, they moved into the house by Mangup-Kalye. By then, Safi was glad to get away from the muddy crowded camp and the gang of local children. And yet, almost immediately, she missed them. Mangup-Kalye was so quiet. The silence lay in wait like a relentlessly watchful beast, and in the pause between hammer strokes, the moments when conversation died, it pounced. In her head Safi knew exactly what it looked like. Its great spined back was the ridges of rock high on Mangup-Kalye, and its eye was a window of emptiness in the furthest outcrop, staring down the valley at them.

Safi was scared of Mangup-Kalye. She knew it

was stupid. She wasn't a baby; she was twelve, old enough to know that there was nothing frightening about a heap of old rocks and trees. But knowing it made no difference. During the day she kept as close as she could to her family, and at night she lay frozen under her quilt in the half-built house, listening to the silence and longing to make a movement, any movement, to break it, but too terrified even to twitch a finger. She woke clenched and aching every morning to the ringing birdsong that only made the silence behind even bigger.

Papa and Mehmed, with Mehmed's brother, Ibrahim, and their cousin, Refat, had petitioned the authorities in Bakhchisaray for months to give them back the land where Grandpa's village had stood. Now these men were helping Papa build the first house at Mangup, and when it was finished, they would work together to build the rest so that their families could come home too. The places where the houses would stand were already carefully staked out along the track up the valley, and the men joked that they had held a picket for the right to several metres of string and four stakes in the ground.

But they hadn't even been granted the right to string and stakes, and so they had simply moved their tents to the valley and started to build. They kept the silence away with jokes and Tatar songs, and political talk that made Safi and Lutfi yawn. They sent Safi this way for wood, that way for stones, the other for cups of black sweet tea. They were tired and dirty and happy from days of digging and hefting blocks and banging in nails, seeing the little house rise under their hands.

"Of course, it would help if we had proper tools and good flat ground to start with," Mehmed said cheerfully. His hair and moustache were powdered with yellowish dust from the building blocks, and he kept sneezing. He squinted along the line of the wall, trying to judge if it was level. Back in Uzbekistan Mehmed had been a teacher, while Refat had worked for the post office. "Oh well. If the walls aren't totally straight, it'll just look more creative. Atishoo!"

"Sneeze any harder and you'll blow them down," Refat said. "And I'd never hear the last of it from Mother. 'Forty-eight years in exile, married for fifty, and what have I got to show for it? A son who won't get married and can't even build a house properly!' Remember when she celebrated her golden wedding anniversary? She spent the whole day complaining that she wasn't in her house in Crimea. 'Just a tiny scrap of roof in the homeland would be enough for your little old mother,' she says. 'Just a corner where I can live, not bothering anyone, quiet as a mouse.'"

Everyone laughed. They were all familiar with the irascible letters Refat's mother wrote to him from Uzbekistan. Safi imagined her to be as huge as Refat but, unlike her son, with a temper to match.

"Hey, Ibrahim." Mehmed nudged his brother. "Why didn't you bring a book about building back to Crimea with you?"

"Mmm." Thin, dreamy Ibrahim didn't take his nose out of the book he was reading. He was studying history and Arabic, and while everyone else, even Mama and Safi, pitched in as much as they could to help, Ibrahim kept getting distracted by anything printed. In the evenings he practised Arabic lettering on the paper cement sacks, and pinned the scraps on the half-built walls so that Safi and Mama and Grandpa had prayers from the Koran over their heads when they went to bed.

Safi thought the lettering was lovely, but she would have preferred a roof to keep out the rain. In Uzbekistan rain had been rare and welcome; when it fell people stood in their doorways holding their hands out and laughing. Here Safi had come to dread the dull tappety-tap of the first drops falling on the plastic sheeting above their heads. "Mama!" she would shriek, and her mother would come running with bowls and buckets and more sheeting that they seemed to be endlessly and hopelessly rearranging to try to keep the beds dry. Safi had never paid such attention to the sky before. She got to know all the variations of rain cloud: grey and lilac and indigo massing behind the spines of Mangup-Kalye. She developed a permanent crick in her neck from gazing upwards so much.

"Hey, Safi, look at him."

"At who?" Safi turned back to Lutfi. She was supposed to be mixing cement with her brother and Ibrahim, but Ibrahim had got engrossed in his book and stopped stirring entirely.

"Ibrahim *Aga*," Safi said loudly.

"Mmm." Ibrahim, sitting on an upturned bucket, made a couple of blind stabs at the cement with the stick and then subsided again. One foot dangled temptingly close to the soggy grey mass.

"Superstar scholar Ibrahim, in the Crimean Tatar Star Alley," Lutfi whispered, scraping up the wet cement so that it settled round the bucket rim and touched Ibrahim's shoe. "How long do you think it'll take to dry?"

Safi looked at how much of his book Ibrahim had left to read. He wasn't yet halfway through. "Oh, I think we've got long enough."

The rest of the cement they took into the cold, damp house, where Papa, Refat and Mehmed were building a crude stove from bricks and metal piping.

Safi looked at it dubiously. It was distinctly wonky. "Is that really going to stay up and keep us warm?"

"Of course. Soon stop your mother from coughing. Where's Ibrahim?"

"He's really busy."

"I bet," Mehmed muttered.

"Oh, don't disturb him…"

The stove was built and it was starting to get dark when there was a shout from outside. Ibrahim had finished his book.

"What the—"

"I don't remember *that* line from the Koran." Refat grinned.

It took half an hour to chip Ibrahim and the bucket free from the cement, and his shoe would never be the same. Mama, coming slowly back from the spring with two buckets of water, stared.

"Whatever are you doing?"

Safi and Lutfi had been in trouble, but now when Mama started laughing they knew they were forgiven. Mama hadn't laughed much recently. It was her idea to make a real Crimean Tatar Star Alley, a row of their footsteps in cement beside the front doorstep: Grandpa first, as the oldest and most respected, and then, in order of size, bear-sized Refat, Mehmed and Papa (who argued about whose feet were bigger until Mama had to arbitrate), Ibrahim ("What, again?"), Lutfi, Mama and Safi, and a space at the end where Lenara's little feet would be.

They all stepped back to admire the result. After some thought, Ibrahim took a stick and wrote an Arabic sentence in the wet cement over the doorway.

"What does it say?"

"Respect your elders, especially when they're scholars hard at work studying." Ibrahim ducked his brother's hand.

"No shirking. Now's the time for building, not books."

"Never trust two children alone with a load of wet cement."

"I'm not a child," Lutfi objected.

"Then don't behave like one," said Papa, but he wasn't really cross.

Ibrahim translated. "It's from the Koran. It says: 'Lord, build for me a home with Thee in the garden ... and deliver me from the unjust people.'"

Safi looked doubtfully at the great bulk of Mangup-Kalye, wondering if this was their garden.

Grandpa nodded approvingly. "Perfect."

The new stove wasn't a huge success. There was no shortage of wood from the slopes of Mangup-Kalye, but Mama had never had to manage a wood-burning stove before, just as the men had never had to build one. It kept going out, and it smoked horribly. The smell got into their hair, their quilts, their few clothes hanging on nails in the stone and mortar walls. Mama's cough changed from a damp chesty one to a dry hacking one that afflicted Grandpa too. Still, it warmed the house a little, and dried out the concrete foundations, so at last they could collect their container that had arrived in Simferopol from Uzbekistan. It fitted snugly in the cellar, and everyone gathered round as Papa opened it up.

Inside were all the things they'd boxed up so

carefully in Samarkand: clothes and shoes, pictures and books and china. Ibrahim's eyes sparkled at the books, but Mama hardly looked at these things, searching through them quickly until she found the packages of pasta, beans, rice, dried fruit and green tea.

"Safi, get the tea things out of that box."

Safi tore herself away from the folded clothes. Mama had always been smartly dressed in Uzbekistan, and the smell of perfume rising out of the container took her straight back to their old house, Mama sitting at her mirror each morning before work, wafting scent bottles under Safi's nose and asking, "Which one today, Safi?"

"That one, the rosy one. It goes with your dress…"

"Quickly, Safinar." Mama had given up waiting for the water to boil on the wood stove, and had lit their stinking little Primus instead. She held out her hands for the teapot and bowls, her thin wrists sticking out from her jumper. Mama hadn't worn perfume since they came to Crimea. Now she smelt of woodsmoke and paraffin and damp.

"Not in here. Lutfi, bring the tray," Papa said. He had a bright, mischievous expression on his face. He guided Mama carefully out of the house and round to the back. "There."

While Mama had been collecting the container with Mehmed, Papa had been busy. Helped by Lutfi and Refat, he had built an open-sided wooden shelter which Grandpa had draped with camouflage netting. The floor of the shelter was about as high off the ground as a bed would be, and Safi and Lutfi had arranged their blankets and quilts on it. In the middle Papa had put a low table, and Safi had filled a jar with snowdrops from the edge of the woods to decorate it. It was a proper *chaykhana*, like at home in Uzbekistan. Now they could sit on quilts and cushions drinking green tea out of shallow bowls, as though everything was all right.

Papa looked at Mama expectantly. Mama gazed at the *chaykhana*. It looked a little lost and lonely in the empty valley.

"What pretty flowers," she said at last. She leant against Papa. "Lutfi, you forgot the sugar."

Papa's fierce, lively face was a little disappointed. He drank his tea with hasty gulps. "Now I know we're home," he said. "Our very own tea, brewed on our very own land, and drunk in our very own *chaykhana*." He kissed Mama on the cheek.

"It isn't our very own land," Mama said tiredly.

"It was ours, and we're making it ours again." Papa's voice was sharp. "Elmira, where's your faith?"

"We met the police on the way back. They stopped us…" Mama looked at Safi. "Safi, go and see if you can find the sugar bowl in the box."

Safi went back to the house reluctantly. She knew she'd been sent out of the way. Mama didn't really want the sugar bowl; she wanted to talk about how things were going wrong. For the first week or so Mama had tried to persuade Safi that it was fun living in the valley, like camping. But camping was only really fun because at the end of it you knew you could go back to your cosy warm house and have a bath and put on clean clothes. Here, there was nowhere to go back to. Mama never said anything outright, but as Safi helped her cook on the awful stove and watched her trying to keep everyone warm and clean, she couldn't help noticing that her mother did not share the cheerful confidence of the men. Papa and the others were so busy building, they didn't seem to notice how cold and lonely and difficult this valley was; what a horrible place to live. And it still didn't belong to them. Papa and

Mehmed were sure that by building on it they could claim the land as theirs, and it was true that so far no one had even come to look at what they were doing. No one ever seemed to come to this valley. The nearest village was half an hour's walk along the road that skirted Mangup-Kalye, and Bakhchisaray was twenty kilometres the other way. The few cars that drove past sometimes slowed, their drivers leaning out to stare, but they never stopped. Why should they? There was nothing here: no village, no people. It was as if the Tatars had been abandoned to the huge brooding silence that was lying in wait right now outside the little *chaykhana* where they sat around the teapot. It was waiting for when the voices and laughter stopped, and then it would pounce.

Safi stirred the contents of an open box. There was no sugar bowl, but nestled among the woolly socks and striped Uzbek scarves she found the shiny brass coffee grinder and coffee pot. She stroked them gently with her finger. They looked so cosy tucked among the bright silk, she longed to climb in and snuggle up beside them. Lenara might still be small enough to do so, but Safi was far too big. With a deep sigh she closed the lid. It felt like home was inside that box, and she couldn't fit in.

The voices from the *chaykhana* had gone quiet. Mehmed and Refat were politely sipping their tea and gazing at nothing in particular. Lutfi looked hunched and unhappy. Grandpa held out his hand. "Come here, Safinar."

Safi's fingers were sore and bruised from lugging around the sharp-edged building blocks, but Grandpa closed his warm, leathery palm round them very gently.

"We've had tea; now it's time for a story," Papa said. He was talking to Grandpa, but his eyes were on Mama. "Tell us about my grandfather, Seit Ahmet. To show how we belong here, and always have, in Adym-Chokrak."

6

SEIT AHMET

*G*randpa began. "My father was born and bred here in Adym-Chokrak, like his father and his father before that. Seit Ahmet was my father's name, and he was the eldest of three brothers. Knew the shape of our valley like his own hand, did Seit Ahmet."

"He knew a week beforehand when snow would fall, and when it would melt in spring," Papa continued. This was a story they had all heard many times. "Then it was time for the shepherds to take the fat-tailed sheep up to the high pastures; time to plant the tobacco field."

"And then all summer to watch the plants grow tall and heady with flowers." Grandpa took up the

62

thread again. "The sheep fattened and the mountain orchards filled with small yellow apples and scarlet pears; the tobacco leaves lay drying in the barn. Adym-Chokrak was where Seit Ahmet was born, and Adym-Chokrak was where he wanted to die. But in between the heart may grow restless, taxes were high, and there were goods to be collected for the *bogcha* Seit Ahmet's sister was embroidering for her marriage."

"What's a *bogcha*?" Lutfi whispered.

"Shh!"

"This was many years ago, when Crimea was part of Russia and ruled by the Russian tsar. When the officers arrived, recruiting for the tsar's army, Seit Ahmet went away to the wars. After five long years he came riding back to Adym-Chokrak, his carbine on his shoulder and his sabre in his belt, and all the girls in the village looked out of their windows to admire his fine moustache and his medals."

"He'd seen the world, and he'd seen the wars," Papa said. "And he found out that there's nowhere in the world as fine as Crimea, and no war worth fighting except the war for home." He was still looking at Mama, and Mama was gently brushing the

63

stiff white skirts of the snowdrops with her finger, and listening.

"Seit Ahmet sat at the edge of the flowering tobacco field, thinking about a certain girl with gold thread in her plaits who had looked very tenderly out of her window as he passed. That was when a messenger rode into the village. 'Seit Ahmet! Your father has three sons, and now the tsar needs your middle brother to serve in his army.'"

"But Seit Ahmet's middle brother was studying in the Zindjirli *medresse*," Safi chimed in, "and he couldn't just leave."

"That's right. Seit Ahmet pondered learning and warfare, family and honour, and at last he said, 'What must be, must be, *inshallah*.' He collected his carbine and his sabre, and once again he rode away to the wars.

"He served for four more years, and when he came back to Adym-Chokrak, all clinking medals and curling moustache, the girls looked out admiringly as he passed, but not quite so admiringly as before, because he wasn't as young as he had been."

"Oh, those girls," Mehmed said, giving Refat a nudge.

"Shh!"

"Seit Ahmet sat at the edge of the field. The tobacco had all been gathered in, and in the distance Ai-Petri Mountain gleamed white with the first snow. He packed his pipe bowl with the sweet fresh tobacco and lay back watching the smoke twirl up into the air. Where's my pipe, by the way?"

"Don't interrupt the story!" several voices cried at once. They'd heard it many times before, but they all loved it.

"Well, all right then. *Ta-ta-tum, ta-ta-tum*, the hoof beats of a messenger came rattling up the valley. 'Seit Ahmet! Your father has three sons, and now the tsar needs your youngest brother to serve in his army.'

"Seit Ahmet's middle brother was a schoolteacher by this time, with a wife from the village who had once worn gold thread in her plaits. But now their youngest brother was studying in the Zindjirli *medresse*. Seit Ahmet lay on the cool Crimean earth and pondered the laws of Islam: honour Allah above all, and His prophet, and next honour the family, the homeland and education. 'What must be, must be, *inshallah*,' said Seit Ahmet, and he rode away a third time to the wars."

"So many wars," Mama murmured.

"He fought for three more years, and he came back with a hole where a bullet had gone right through him. When he rode into the village he said, 'I'm an old bachelor of thirty-eight; what girl will look at me now?'"

"Those heartless girls." Mehmed nudged Refat again. Refat was in his thirties, and his mother was always on at him to get married.

"Wait till the end of the story," Safi said. That was her favourite bit.

"Seit Ahmet sat at the edge of the freshly ploughed tobacco field, and he said, 'I've fought alongside the Russians against many different countries, and all I've learnt is that none of them keep the promises they make to us. I've learnt that there's nowhere in the world finer than Crimea, and there's no one to love and defend Crimea but us Crimean Tatars.'

"'And one day perhaps we'll die for Crimea; but for the moment, how about helping me plant this field instead of sitting there philosophizing like a great lump?' said a voice behind him.

"My father jumped half out of his skin to see a young girl, not eighteen if she was a day, in the field with a bag of seeds tied round her waist. When he had returned to Adym-Chokrak before, the girls had stayed at home, peeking out through their windows at the world and the handsome soldiers riding by, waiting for a husband to come courting. Yet here now was a girl out in the field frowning and smiling at him, pretty as a painting and bold as brass. Seit Ahmet felt his stern heart stirring, and wondered if thirty-eight was perhaps, after all, not so very old. Ah, what must be, must be, *inshallah*!"

"And that was my great-grandmother!" said Safi.

"She was a fighter too," Grandpa said. "And sometimes she fought with Seit Ahmet, but never over the things that really matter."

"What matters is Crimea," Papa said to Mama.

Grandpa looked at him. "My mother knew that what really matters is kindness. One day I'll tell you a story about that too."

7

WHO LIVED THERE?

Safi woke up to a strange new brightness. When she looked, the other two beds in the house, where Mama and Grandpa slept, were already empty. Safi pulled the quilt up almost to her eyes and peeked overhead, frightened that the plastic sheeting had blown away in the night. But the pale morning light was slanting in through the window; the boards fixed over it had gone. When she wriggled out of bed and went outside she discovered why. Lutfi was painting on them. The big red letters spelt out the unfinished message: REBUILD OUR ANCIENT TATAR V—

Refat was working on a second board. His read: RECAIM OUR CRIMEAN TATAR LAND!

"What are you doing?" Safi yawned and shivered, her toes curling in the damp grass.

"Put some shoes on," Refat said distractedly. His broad, high-cheekboned face was anxious, and he was trying to put the missing 'L' into 'RECAIM' so it wasn't too noticeable.

"Yes, but what are you doing?"

"Protesting," Lutfi said. "Down by the pond." He sounded pleased, probably because at last something different was happening in their monotonous valley.

"Put some shoes on first!" Refat called after her as she went to investigate.

There was a police car parked by the pond. Three policemen were standing in front of it. Opposite them stood Safi's parents and grandfather with Mehmed, in tense silence.

"What's happening?" Safi slipped her hand into her mother's, and Mama jumped; she hadn't heard her approach.

"Safi! Go back to the house at once."

One of the policemen turned and spat on the ground. "You'd even bring your filthy brats into this. You should be ashamed."

Papa made a sharp movement, but Mehmed put a hand on his arm.

69

"Our children fight our fight," Grandpa said. "For our homeland, our country."

"Poor kid looks half starved," said another policeman. "Hasn't even got any shoes. Bet you'd rather go home, wouldn't you, little girl, instead of living here like gypsies."

"Like beggars. Why did you have to come back? What was wrong with Uzbekistan or wherever you've come from?"

It was on the tip of Safi's tongue to say there was nothing wrong with Uzbekistan; it was much nicer than this miserable Crimea. But her parents were listening. Instead she said timidly, "But we always lived here."

She looked to Grandpa for support, and he said, "Crimea's our home."

"We Russians always lived here too. And it was you who betrayed us to the German fascists!"

"Traitors."

"Safi, *go back to the house*."

Mama fairly pushed Safi back the way she had come. Past the pond she met Lutfi running down. He'd nailed a post onto the back of the board to make a notice: REBUILD OUR ANCIENT TATAR VILLAGE!

"Are they going to arrest us?" Safi asked anxiously.

"They can't," Lutfi said. "They'd have to arrest ten thousand of us, all over Crimea. There's no law any more that says the Tatars can't come back. They're just going to have to put up with us." He ran on, pushed the post into the soft chalky ground by the roadside and stood by it defiantly.

The police didn't arrest anyone, but they didn't go away. They sat in their car, and Refat and Mehmed sat down by Lutfi's sign, and they stared at each other. Lutfi stayed with them for a bit, until he got bored because nothing was happening and went to make more signs with Ibrahim instead. Ibrahim's notices were in Arabic.

"What do they say?" Lutfi asked.

"Get lost, Russian occupiers, I hope."

"I don't think that line's in the Koran either…"

When two days later the police turned up again and sat there glowering, Mehmed drove Mama, Papa and Grandpa to Bakhchisaray to try to talk to the local administration. Ibrahim sat down by the signs, with a book to read. Refat pottered around the outside of the house fixing and tidying, for all the world like a proud housewife. The walls of yellow blocks were so high now that Safi couldn't reach the top of them standing on tiptoe, and there were several windows. All of the men, even Lutfi, were so proud you would think they were building a palace. But every time she looked at it, Safi just thought about the house they'd left behind in Samarkand, surrounded by its bright sunlit garden, and remembered her own room where she'd actually undressed before going to bed, not like here where they all put on extra clothes to keep warm at night. She longed for that lost cosiness and safety, for a roof over her head.

Refat noticed her glum expression, and told Safi to go and explore.

"Where to?" she asked dismally.

"The caves. They're famous, older than even the Tatars. Churches and mosques and kenessas, wine cellars and all sorts – a whole city."

"What are kenessas?"

"Karaim places of worship."

"Who lived there?"

Refat gestured vaguely. "Someone. Everyone... Ages ago."

Since they had arrived, Safi had been no further

up the valley than to the spring. None of them had. They'd been too busy building. Safi had hardly noticed the snowdrops withering away, and starry yellow flowers with pointed petals taking their place in the grass around the tents and *chaykhana*. Now she looked along the track doubtfully. Round the corner, she knew, she'd be in sight of the eye in the rock.

"Off you go," Refat said encouragingly as he set off towards the pond. "Don't get lost, mind. Take Lutfi with you."

Lutfi was in a bad mood. Safi was the only one who knew why; he'd been hoping to go to Bakhchisaray as well, to post a letter he'd written to his girlfriend, Larissa, in Samarkand. Safi found him sulking in the house, reading over the closely scrawled pages.

"Maybe there's a post office in the next village," Safi offered, after a while of sitting with him in sympathetic silence. "You can always ask Refat." She was trying to make Lutfi laugh; Refat's daily letters to his mother, and her grumpy answers that she sent via friends in Bakhchisaray, were legendary.

"When am I going to get a chance to go there," Lutfi growled, "when we're so busy building this hovel?" All his enthusiasm for the house had disappeared. He aimed a kick at the wall, and a chunk of mortar fell out from between the stones.

"Larissa will wait for your letter; she won't mind."

"What do you know about it?" Lutfi hunched his shoulders away from her, ignoring her hurt face.

This was so unfair. Safi was the only one who knew about Larissa, and she knew because she'd carried messages between them and covered up for Lutfi when he was out with her instead of at the sports club or Tatar language classes. Papa and especially Grandpa didn't approve of Lutfi meeting Russian girls; they wanted him to find a good Crimean Tatar girlfriend, and he hadn't been allowed out late even with a Tatar girl. They didn't understand love.

Lutfi seemed to realize he'd been mean, because after a moment he turned back to Safi and pulled one of her plaits. "What d'you want then?"

"Refat said you should come with me exploring up the mountain."

"To those old caves?" Lutfi looked through his letter one last time, with his sad faraway face on, and then put it in his pocket. "All right."

Along the track past the spring they came to a

chalky path leading off to the right into the woods and up between two of the ridges of rock.

"Let's go this way." Safi was anxious to get off the track, away from the eye in the furthest outcrop.

Lutfi peered up the path sceptically. "I suppose it goes to the top. Have you noticed, Safi, that in all Grandpa's stories about the village, he never talks about Mangup-Kalye?"

Safi pondered this as they walked into the wood. She knew all about the houses in Adym-Chokrak, the fountain and the mosque, the tobacco field where Seit Ahmet had met her great-grandmother; she knew so much that she'd always thought when they came back to it, she'd be able to make her way around as if she'd lived there all her life. But about where this path went to, she knew nothing.

"You're right. And now the village has disappeared, but the mountain is left." She glanced up at the slopes above – a spiteful look. "Maybe that's why I don't like it. It shouldn't be here. It's not fair that it's still here."

"Don't you like it? It's just a mountain."

"It's spooky." Safi tried not to sound too serious, because it was silly to be scared by a mountain, she knew.

75

Lutfi gave her a quizzical look. "Nutty little sister. It's not spooky. It's just boring. This whole flipping valley is so boring: no one around; nowhere to go."

It wasn't exactly a mountain, Safi realized as they walked on. Their valley lay deep between high grey plateaux of rock. The spines of Mangup-Kalye were really more like the knuckles of four great fingers digging into the wooded slopes. The whole of Mangup was a clenched fist, and they were walking up between the first and second knuckle.

"Lutfi, what did Mama say about the police when she came back from Simferopol with the container?"

"I'm not supposed to tell you."

Safi just waited. She knew he would; Lutfi was hopeless at keeping secrets from her.

"She and Mehmed got stopped by the police from Krasniy Mak." That was the village on the other side of Mangup. "The same ones who are sitting by the pond now. They asked to see our residence permits, but they must have known we don't have any. Mama told them we've applied in Bakhchisaray and are just waiting for a decision, but the police said we'd never get permission and we'll be sent back to Uzbekistan by the end of the month."

"They can't send us back!" Along with the shock, Safi was ashamed to feel a nudge of hope. Wouldn't it be wonderful to go back to their lovely house, and Lenara, and Jemile... But they'd sold the house in Samarkand.

"Of course they can't." Safi thought Lutfi sounded slightly regretful. He had left behind lots of friends too, as well as Larissa. "They just want to scare us by making pathetic threats and sitting on their fat backsides by the pond. The Russians have been trying to scare the Tatars away from Crimea for over two hundred years, ever since they first invaded; they've always wanted it for themselves." Lutfi kicked a stone, scowling. "Stupid police. Papa was angry with Mama for even being upset about them."

"They never used to argue, did they?"

"No."

Overhead the trees had tiny buds clinging to their smooth grey branches, and shining drops of water from the morning's rain. The birds sang and sang, as if desperate to fill the silence, but they couldn't; they only made it echo larger than ever. The path zigzagged steeply between tree roots and big stones padded with moss. The air smelt green.

"Even if I could send the letter to Larissa, she

couldn't reply anyway," Lutfi grumbled as they climbed. "Where would she send it to? Poky Little Valley Miles from Anywhere Under a Mountain?"

"Adym-Chokrak."

"But Adym-Chokrak doesn't exist any more, does it? Look at a map of Crimea. There's nothing marked here except for Mangup-Kalye and the caves."

"Refat said there was a whole city up at the top."

"With a cafe where we can get a drink, thank goodness. I need it." Lutfi was panting from the steep climb.

"Daft."

"There is. Refat said. Best drinks in Crimea. I can't wait, I'm really thirsty, aren't you?"

"I've got no money," Safi said doubtfully.

"I'll buy you something. What would you like? They've got Tatar tonic, Karaim cola, Russian rum and vodka, Ukrainian, um, unicycles…"

"You—!"

Lutfi dodged her thump. "Of course, it's totally staffed by the ghosts of whoever lived in this city…"

They came to two long trailing stems of ivy laid across the path in front of them, as if to say, *No further*. Beyond, the ground was alight with pale yellow flowers growing thickly among scattered gravestones.

They halted. The graves were everywhere, tumbled among the tree roots, leaning at crazy angles and green with moss. They were shaped like narrow stone beds with high ends carved deep with writing. The thousands of flowers glowed like lamps on the ground under the trees, lighting up this still, secret cemetery.

"I guess we've found who lived here," Lutfi said quietly. "Do you think they're Tatars? They don't look like Muslim graves. I don't recognize this writing."

"Let's go back," Safi said. Her voice trembled.

She turned to retrace her steps, and Lutfi followed.

"Is that why Grandpa never talks about Mangup?" he wondered as they thudded downwards, knees aching from the steepness. "Let's ask him. Maybe it really is haunted."

Safi shrugged. "They're just graves." She wished they had never found them.

8

EMPTY BEDS

The Bakhchisaray authorities refused even to see Papa and Grandpa. But while they waited in corridors and knocked on doors at the town hall, Mama had been to one of the schools. She'd met the director and somehow managed to arrange for Safi to attend classes, even though the whole family lacked residence permits.

Papa teased her about it. "We should have sent you to the authorities to get the rights to the land, instead of picketing for months. Trust a woman to get exactly what she wants in one afternoon." But Safi could see he was really quite annoyed. He wanted his children to help rebuild a Tatar Crimea before going off to get a Russian education. "We'll open proper Tatar schools, or at least classes, in Crimea soon," he said. "Then they can go to school."

Mama was adamant. In Bakhchisaray she'd also called Jemile's mother and talked to Lenara, who was staying at their house. There were still tears in her eyes when she got back to the valley, and she wasn't in the mood for teasing or arguing. "It's not right for Safi to be stuck here all the time: the only girl, the only child. She helps as much as she can, but she's still young, and you know an education's important, Russian or Ukrainian or Tatar. If we're going to live here, we'll have to try and fit in with the local people. Lutfi really should go as well."

"Lutfi stays and works on the house. We need him."

"Flipping house," Lutfi muttered, too low for anyone except Safi to hear. But he looked a bit proud too, because Papa had said he was needed, like a man. Lutfi had never been much interested in school anyway, except as a place to meet friends, and in Samarkand Papa had often shouted at him about his grades.

"All right then, until it's built." Mama clearly understood there was no point arguing about Lutfi. "But I insist on Safi going now, at least a couple of

81

days a week. There's a school bus from Krasniy Mak. It goes right past here, so we can arrange for it to stop for her."

"Well, we'll try it. Just as long as I don't see my daughter behaving like a Russian schoolgirl." Papa gave in with a short laugh.

Despite their failure at the town hall, Papa and Mehmed had returned in a fiercely jubilant mood, because the authorities had finally granted permission for the Tatars from the Bakhchisaray camp to build houses. There was going to be a big meeting in Simferopol in two days' time to celebrate, and to demand the same rights for the other squatter settlements like their own. They talked excitedly about it all evening. No one seemed to want to discuss Safi's school any more. She sat in the corner and worried. What was she going to wear? Would she have learnt completely different things in Uzbekistan, and be way behind the other children? Would they like her?

At last it was Refat who noticed. He came to sit beside her. "So, did you go up on Mangup-Kalye? What did you find?"

"A cemetery," Safi said glumly. She didn't really want to be reminded of those tombstones, mossy

82

and tumbled on their cold carpet of flowers.

But Refat was interested. "I wonder who's buried there. Let's ask your grandfather about it."

Grandpa was silent for a long time, and Safi wondered if he was angry at their questions. The ivy tendrils across the path had been a warning, a sign to keep out.

"We didn't go in," she said. "We weren't expecting to find it."

"My best friend once came looking for my grave there," said Grandpa.

Safi went cold. She was glad when Refat pointed out, "But you're not dead, Ismail *Aga*."

"But I was so far away, so gone without a trace, I might as well have been." Grandpa's gaze was distant, turned back to a painful past. "My friend Ayder came from the war to find us, but he was too late, and we had all gone."

"You mean Ayder *Aga*?" Safi remembered him, a crumpled, sad-eyed man who had often come to visit Grandpa in Samarkand before he died.

"Was he in the Red Army?" Ibrahim asked.

"That's right. He defended the Soviet Union against the Germans. Alongside him fought Russians and Chechens, Ukrainians and Uzbeks, Azeris and Armenians. It didn't matter. They were all from the Soviet Union. They all wanted the same thing: to get the German fascists out of their country so they could return to their families; to stay alive.

"Ayder was in Azerbaijan with his unit when an Azeri officer, a Muslim like him, said he should go back to Crimea as fast as he could. He said he'd heard something about the Crimean Tatars, and he'd help Ayder get leave to go home before it was too late. But he didn't say what it might be too late for.

"It was June 1944; Crimea had just been liberated from the Germans when Ayder arrived, met by the smell of roses. The flags welcoming the returning Red Army hung limp in the streets. Everywhere walls were shattered by bullets and bombs. From lamp posts dangled the stiff, dry bodies of collaborators."

"Hanged?" Lutfi asked, goggle-eyed. Grandpa seemed not to hear.

"At his mother's house in Akmesjit, the door was locked. Next door was empty too. There were no Tatar children playing in the yard. It was as if they had all stepped out for something, and if he waited they would come back. But he did wait, and no one came. Ayder was wearing his uniform, which made him look like any other soldier defending the Soviet Union, but the Russians and Ukrainians avoided his eye, and hurried away when he approached. All through the city was the same. The Tatar houses stood deserted; when he peered through the windows he could see the kind of mess people leave when they are in a hurry and expect to be back soon to tidy up.

"My friend thought perhaps the Tatars had fled the fighting and gone to the villages for refuge. So he came out here, to Adym-Chokrak. But here too, all he found was empty houses and silence, and up on Mangup-Kalye he found a cemetery. It wasn't a Tatar cemetery, but there was nowhere else to look, nowhere else we could be. Ayder searched there for his family, for my grave, my mother's grave, the graves of all the vanished Crimean Tatars."

The silence of those narrow stone beds up on the hillside. Imagine the silence of a whole village emptied of people, the beds in the houses unslept in and stony cold. Safi wished more than ever that they'd never found the graveyard.

"But you weren't buried there, *Khartbaba*," she said.

"No. And it was our Karaim neighbour who told Ayder what had happened."

"It's a Karaim graveyard, and there's one of their kenessas up on Mangup," Mehmed said. "The Karaim people are so old no one knows where they came from. They've been in Crimea even longer than the Tatars."

"Old Gulnara *Tata* tended the graveyard on Mangup, even though no one remembers who is buried there any more. She found my friend there, crying as he searched, and she told him, 'They took all the Crimean Tatars away. Red Army soldiers, like you. Some people say they drowned them in the Caspian Sea, or took them to Siberia.'

"She went on cleaning the moss from the gravestones. That's almost all that's left of the Karaims in Crimea: their tombs, and the empty cave cities. 'Sometimes it's a good thing to have no real homeland,' Gulnara *Tata* said to Ayder. 'No one cares about us any more.'"

There was no sound in the little house but the paraffin lamp's faint hiss. Everyone was listening to the story now.

"How did Ayder find you again?" Lutfi asked at last.

"He had nothing but his army uniform and his soldier's papers. He went back to his unit, and a few months later he was sent west to the Front. He was with the Red Army when it marched into Berlin."

Mehmed thumped the wall with his fist. "He was fighting the Germans when the Soviet authorities said he had betrayed this country to them."

"He had always thought he was the same as all the other soldiers, wanting only to free their homeland and return to their families. But while he'd been struggling to stay alive, the Soviets had taken away his homeland and given it to the Russians," Grandpa said. "After the war, he too was exiled to Uzbekistan. He kept on searching, and in 1950 he found me and my mother. His own family vanished for ever. He never even found their graves."

9

YOU CAN'T LIVE IN
DREAMS FOR EVER

*S*chool was wonderfully familiar. As she stepped
through the doorway into a green-painted hall
smelling of cabbage, Safi felt for the first time in
Crimea that she was in a place she knew. It was just
like her school in Samarkand: there were the rows
of faded black and white photographs of war heroes
on the walls; there were even exactly the same old
Soviet notices about Keeping Clean and Working
Hard and Growing Up to Become a Good Communist. It was several months since the Soviet Union
had finally collapsed and Uzbekistan and Ukraine
had become different countries, but no one seemed
to have told the teachers in Bakhchisaray that.

The children milling about and shouting looked

pretty much the same too, although there were no Uzbeks with their close-cropped black heads. Safi watched them shyly, wondering which ones might become her friends. She couldn't understand why Papa had made a fuss about Russian and Ukrainian girls, when back in Samarkand she'd gone to school with Russians and Uzbeks and no one had said anything. But the best thing happened when she got to her class.

"Safinar Ismailova." The teacher read out her name rather disapprovingly. "You'd better sit next to Ayshe. No doubt you'll get along."

Safi went to her seat eagerly. She knew at once from the name that Ayshe was Tatar too.

Ayshe smiled. She had black hair in a long ponytail, and was wearing a beautifully pressed dress. "Where are you from?" she whispered.

"Uzbekistan."

"Me too. We came to Crimea two years ago. My father managed to buy a house in Bakhchisaray."

"Oh, you're so lucky." Safi felt wildly envious, and suddenly rather self-conscious next to Ayshe's tidy dress and glossy ponytail. Mama had dug out her old school clothes from the container, steaming the creases out over the boiling kettle before hanging them carefully on the end of one of the beds overnight. The result wasn't entirely successful. "We've been here just a few weeks. We're still building our house."

"That explains—" Ayshe broke off suddenly.

"What?"

"Oh, nothing." Ayshe had her hand up over her nose but now she dropped it. "Shh. We'll get told off."

Safi sat through a pleasantly easy maths lesson and half a history lesson before she realized. There was a smell in the air, a sort of damp, scorched smell. She peered under the desk, and furtively over her shoulder, and then her heart lurched as if someone had thrown a large stone at her chest. It was coming from her. In the stuffy warmth of the classroom, all the dirt and smoke from their horrible stove was oozing out of her clothes. Back at Adym-Chokrak she was so used to the smoke she hardly noticed it any more. Now it seemed like the most overpoweringly awful smell in the world. Safi's cheeks and ears burned. She hunched down in her seat and wished for a disaster. A fire, a revolution, the end of the world – anything to get her out of there.

Ayshe caught her eye and gave her a rueful,

sympathetic smile. "It's OK," she murmured encouragingly. "It's not that bad."

Somehow that just made Safi feel even worse. There were still twenty minutes till the end of the lesson. She picked up her book and hid her flaming face behind it, trying to concentrate on the bit of text they were supposed to be reading.

It was about the partisans in the Second World War; guerrilla fighters who had fought against the Germans when they occupied Crimea. It reminded Safi of Grandpa's friend Ayder, and other stories too. She frowned at the book, forgetting her clothes, and nudged Ayshe.

"What?"

"Look. This book's wrong."

"Safinar." The teacher was glaring at her over his glasses. "Would you like to share whatever you're whispering about with the whole class?"

"Sorry, sir. It was nothing."

"I'm sure it was something. Perhaps you've found an error in the textbook that you'd like to correct, hmm?" The teacher had a sarcastic grin. "Do let us hear the Crimean Tatar version."

Safi bit her lip. She wanted to put her head down and pretend she was a nice ordinary schoolgirl like the others. But she'd always been told she should be proud of being Crimean Tatar, and that meant she couldn't back down. "It's a question, sir. There's a list of partisans here who fought in Crimea in the war. But there are only Russians on it. I was wondering where the Crimean Tatars are. I know they fought too."

"Oh, you know that, do you?" The teacher was suddenly at her side, snatching the book out of her hand.

"Yes. My grandfather's cousin—"

"This book was written by respected historians," the teacher snapped, "while you are an uneducated little barbarian, and entirely wrong. If you disrupt this class any more I'll send you home. Do you have anything else to say?"

"But… It's a Soviet textbook, sir," Safi said haltingly.

"What's that got to do with it?"

"Nothing, sir," she whispered.

"She's right, sir," said a voice behind her. Safi peeked round. A boy sitting near the back had his hand up. "There were Tatar partisans. My grandfather was one too."

"Yes," Ayshe chimed in.

Just then the bell rang. At once the classroom filled with the sound of scraping chairs as the other children rushed out for lunch, although some lingered to watch the new girl get into trouble. The teacher stayed by Safi's desk, tapping the book against his palm and studying her and Ayshe and the boy at the back.

"I grew up in the Soviet Union with this textbook," he said at last, in a different, somehow less teacherly voice. "In those days, we always believed what we were told. What makes you think you can tell me what is and isn't true?"

"My grandpa said—" Safi began, and at the same time the boy at the back said, "The Crimean Tatars—"

"I know, you think the whole of Crimea belongs to you." The teacher suddenly slammed the book down on the desk. "Get out of here, and don't you dare disrupt my lesson again."

Outside the classroom, the boy grinned at her. "My name's Rustem. Good one, Safinar." And Ayshe squeezed her hand and said, "Hey, will you come to tea sometime? Sometime soon? I'll ask my parents."

Safi beamed. She had friends. Ayshe and Rustem

weren't as good as Jemile, of course, but they were a million times better than no one. They were better than any disaster to get her through the rest of the day in her stinking clothes.

On the bus home after school she watched out of the window anxiously, so as not to miss the pea-green pond at the bottom of the valley where she should get off. She was too shy to meet the looks of any of the other children, although she knew they were staring at her.

At last the bus rounded a corner and she recognized the big rocks on the other side of the road. She got up and made her way to the front.

"Please can you stop."

The driver took no notice.

"Please can you stop for me here, by the pond," she said, louder.

The bus actually seemed to speed up, and she grabbed the back of a seat to stop herself falling over. She knew perfectly well the whole busload was watching her.

"Remember, my father agreed with you this morning that you'd drop me off here. At Adym-Chokrak, the village."

"There's no village here," the driver snapped

without turning round. "Now sit down."

"But—"

"*Sit down!*"

Defeated, Safi stumbled back to her seat. The whole bus was snickering.

"Stupid Tatar."

"Serves you right."

"It's our bus. Why should it stop for you?"

Something hit the back of her head, not hard, but enough to mess up her hair. "Stinky Tatar."

At Krasniy Mak Safi hurried away from the bus stop. She'd have to walk all the way to the valley now, and Mama would want to know why she hadn't got off by the pond. The road was deserted, running deeply between trees. From here, Mangup-Kalye looked quite different; it was a high, unbroken wall of rock rising above the woods, dotted with the black holes of caves. She realized from this side she was seeing the hard edge of the fist.

Halfway along she met Mama, walking at her usual swift, elegant pace to meet her.

"I saw the bus go past. Why didn't you get off by the pond?"

"I missed the place. And the driver forgot." Safi avoided her mother's eye. She knew if she said that the driver had refused to stop, there'd be no more school for her, and she didn't want that.

Mama let it pass. "So how was it?"

"It was great, except… Oh, Mama, you've got to do something about my clothes!"

Safi launched into an impassioned account of the awful smell. She was looking at Mama for sympathy as she talked, but then she faltered. Mama's way of walking was the same as ever, but instead of her old smart clothes she was wearing a grubby coat pulled tight, and boots that had split across one toe. There was no make-up round her eyes to hide the dark shadows of tiredness. No sweet drift of perfume to mask the woodsmoke and damp. A few days ago Mama had marched into the school director's office, knowing exactly how she smelt and looked, and somehow persuaded him to take Safi in school. You would never guess to look at her now that back in Uzbekistan, Mama had had a job much more important than head teacher; she'd been deputy director of a whole district health department.

Safi felt silly and small. "Oh, well," she finished lamely. "Maybe we can air them outside or something."

"I'll wash them this evening," Mama said shortly.

"And get the men to look at the stove again. How were your classes?"

"Fine, except I had an argument with the history teacher."

"On your first day? Oh, Safi."

"I couldn't help it. We were learning about the partisans in the war, and there wasn't anything about Crimean Tatars. So I asked why not, because I know Grandpa's cousin was a partisan, and lots of others."

"If you'd asked that question five years ago in the Soviet Union you'd have been expelled," Mama said. "You weren't expelled, were you?"

"Of course not!" Safi wasn't sure if Mama was joking. "The teacher told me I was wrong, that's all, and I said I was right, and then Rustem and Ayshe joined in and agreed with me."

"Who are Rustem and Ayshe?"

The rest of the way back to the valley passed quickly as Safi told her mother about the two Tatar children.

"So can I go to tea with Ayshe? Can I?"

"I don't see why not, if she's Tatar." Mama ruffled Safi's hair lightly. "You miss your friends, don't you? Back in Samarkand I hardly saw you, you were always out and about with them."

"I especially miss Jemile. And Lenara." They were back by the pond, the entrance to their narrow valley, and Safi felt her heart sinking under the weight of green silence. There wasn't even the sound of building today, and the familiar red car was missing, because the men had driven to the Simferopol meeting.

"And I miss them too, but at least here I've got you to myself." Mama gave her an affectionate pat. "There'll be lots of children for you to play with soon, when the permits are granted and the houses are built; all the Crimean Tatars will send for their families. And now, about that bus. Did the driver really forget?" She looked at Safi's face. "I didn't think so."

"He wouldn't stop. He said there was no village here. But Mama…" Safi clutched her mother's sleeve anxiously. "Please don't tell Papa or Grandpa. I want to keep going to school. I don't mind walking from Krasniy Mak."

"I never knew you were so keen on lessons," Mama teased, although her smile was rather half-hearted. "You just want to abandon me to do all the cooking on my own, is that it?"

"I don't like this valley," Safi said. As soon as it was out of her mouth she tried to correct herself, because it sounded so disloyal to Grandpa and the village that had filled her dreams for as long as she could remember. "I mean, I'm sure I will like it, when the house is built and everything. It's just … it's just… I didn't think everything would be gone. It's not what I was expecting."

"Life's rarely what you expect, Safi. You can hope and you can dream, but in the end life's something you build out of bricks and earth and sweat and tears." Mama looked at her rather sternly. "Even life in Crimea. You can't live in your grandfather's dreams for ever. All right, the bus driver is our secret. Lutfi can walk you there and back from Krasniy Mak."

When he returned with Mehmed that evening, Lutfi was buzzing from the meeting in Simferopol: thousands of Tatars holding up the traffic and taking over the main square outside the Crimean Cabinet of Ministers, buoyed by their victory in Bakhchisaray and more determined than ever to continue their peaceful campaign and press the rest of their demands.

"There are so many of us back in Crimea now,

they have to listen to us," he exulted. "Resettlement on all the old Tatar sites. Tatar representatives in the Crimean parliament. Crimean Tatar schools."

"At school today—"

Lutfi didn't even notice she'd spoken. "Crimean Tatar language to be the official language alongside Ukrainian and Russian…"

"But you can't really speak Tatar," Safi said. "Neither can I." Most of the demands she had been hearing all her life, because as long as she could remember, Papa had campaigned for the right to return to Crimea – always away from home at meetings, taking petitions to Moscow, once even in prison. But she had never heard the demand about language before.

"I'll learn." Lutfi wasn't to be sidetracked. "There was no need to know it while we were in Uzbekistan, but we're back in our own country now. Why should we have to speak the language of those stupid Russians and Ukrainians? They should learn ours. Crimea isn't theirs, it belongs to us."

Lutfi was on fire with enthusiasm. In Simferopol they'd stood shoulder to shoulder, cheering the speakers, seeing the scared look on the Russians' faces and knowing they would win. Safi regarded him sadly. In Uzbekistan she'd lied to Mama and Papa so that Lutfi could skive off Tatar language classes and meet Larissa instead. She hadn't minded, because she'd do anything for her brother and it was exciting being involved, even at a remove, in a real romance. Now it looked as if Lutfi was forgetting all about that.

"Did you post your letter to Larissa?" she whispered to him when they went to bed.

Lutfi got a sudden stricken look. "I... There wasn't a chance to. We were so busy at the meeting. If you'd been there, you'd know what I mean."

"Never mind," Safi said. "I expect you can post it in Krasniy Mak tomorrow." She knew Lutfi hadn't missed the chance. She knew he'd forgotten.

10

HOW KHATIJE JOINED
THE PARTISANS

Safi didn't really mean to tell Papa about the argument with her history teacher, but a few days later it came out anyway.

"You see?" Papa rounded on Mama. "They'll just teach my daughter lies at that school. She'll learn Russian values, Russian morals —"

"She's my daughter too," Mama said sharply. "And she can tell the difference between truth and lies."

Safi was a little frightened of Papa when he was in a mood like this. She had to steel herself to ask, "What do you mean, Russian morals? You never said that about my old school, and there were lots of Russians there."

"In the Soviet Union no one could talk about

their beliefs," Papa said. "It was banned, just like the truth. But we're Muslim and always have been, and that means girls should be modest. Not like those Russian hussies: short skirts, smoking, boys—"

"Asim." Mama spoke quietly, but in a tone Safi had never heard from her before. "If you want your daughter's skirt to be longer, perhaps you should buy her a new one."

There was no money for clothes; Safi knew that perfectly well. There wasn't even enough for things like sugar and toothpaste. All the money went into the building: the wooden beams for the ceiling, glass for the windows, plaster for the walls. It was looking a bit more like a proper house these days, with a sturdy floor and even a door between the kitchen and the next room. Unfortunately the hinges must have dropped, because it didn't shut properly. Mama went through it now, pulling it to behind her, and it scraped along the floor and then stuck.

For a moment, Papa looked as though he was going to stride after her. Then he checked himself and subsided onto a stool instead with a short, angry laugh.

"Women!" he said. "Girls!" he added, reaching over to tug one of Safi's plaits with fierce affection.

"Who'd have them! Are you really so desperate for a new skirt, Safi?"

"It was *you...*" Safi began indignantly, but Papa, with one of his abrupt changes of mood, was laughing at her.

"I remember a story about a skirt," he said, "and it's one you can tell to your history teacher, because it's about how Grandpa's cousin Khatije joined the partisans. Eh, Father?"

Grandpa put down his teacup. "I was thinking of another story," he said, in his slow voice. "About how you came to join the Tatar national movement, Asim."

"I don't know that one." Safi found it hard to imagine that Papa had ever *not* been in the Tatar national movement. "What happened?"

Papa looked at Grandpa. There was a flush of colour across his cheekbones. "Now then."

"Your father," Grandpa said to Safi, "was much more interested in girls than politics. And one fine day he ended up in the middle of a protest march in Uzbekistan by accident, because he followed a girl there. Quite the hero, Asim. He saved the girl from a police beating, and she shouted at him all the way home for it. Elmira was ready to die then; whatever it would take for the Tatars to return to Crimea."

"And that was Mama?" Safi was fascinated by this glimpse of her parents when they were young.

But Papa got up from the stool and said, "That's enough now." Still looking a little flushed, he gently eased the ill-fitting door open and went through to the other room, pulling it closed just as gently behind him.

Grandpa held out a hand to Safi. "I think we should go for a walk."

They left the house to Mama and Papa, because even with the new door there was not much privacy. Safi hoped they weren't still arguing.

"So was the way Khatije joined the partisans like the way Papa joined the nationalist movement?"

"A little. I suppose they are both love stories. But my cousin Khatije was in love with a boy called Abdul, and if Khatije is our pride, then Abdul is our shame."

They had wandered past the pond to the camp-fire Ibrahim had lit to keep himself warm. The men took it in turns to sit by their protest signs, because if they didn't the police or locals kicked them down.

Ibrahim glanced up as Grandpa and Safi held out their chilled fingers to the flames. "Come to keep me company?"

"*Khartbaba's* telling a story."

"Oh, good." Ibrahim carefully laid his pen and notebook aside. Stories were among the few things that could tear him away from his studies.

"My cousin Khatije was a bit older than me. She was a big, brave, laughing girl until she met Abdul." Grandpa smiled to himself. You could see that he had been very fond of his cousin. "Abdul's family had sent him from Akmesjit—"

"That's Simferopol now," Ibrahim put in, for Safi's benefit.

"—to live in our village when the war broke out. He had dewy black eyes and mincing city ways that would make you puke, but I suppose no one had ever kissed Khatije's fingers before and told her she smiled like the sun coming out. The trouble was, in the next breath Abdul told her she was just a stupid dirty village girl. Khatije should have punched him. Instead she went around with a face longer than a summer's day in Ramadan."

"Pig," Safi said.

"So we had enough reason not to like Abdul, but we put up with him until the Germans occupied Crimea. They were very charming, those German soldiers, with their clean pink hands and their downy hair. Abdul liked them at once. He was one of the first to volunteer for the Tatar self-defence brigades the Germans set up, because it meant he could march around in a nice new uniform shouting orders and lording it over the rest of us."

"He wasn't the only one to volunteer," Ibrahim said. "You know how the Soviet authorities treated the Crimean Tatars even before the war, Safi. For ten years they arrested the brightest, the richest, the cleverest, the best. The occupying Germans promised freedom, wealth, our own country again. A chance to get our own back. A lot of Tatars believed them."

Safi was confused. She knew that the reason the Crimean Tatars had been exiled was because the Soviets said they had sided with the Germans in the war. All her life she'd been told that was a lie. But now it sounded as if it was true after all.

"I don't understand about the self-defence what-sits," she said plaintively.

"Brigades. They were like a small local army of Tatars, given weapons and uniforms by the Germans to help fight the Soviet partisans. Sometimes they truly defended us, because the partisans were not always decent, honourable heroes either. But mostly Abdul's brigade had fun. Abdul could requisition whatever he wanted from whoever he liked – or rather, didn't like. He could clear whole villages just by a whisper of collaboration with the partisans."

"What do you mean, clear?"

"I mean destroy," Grandpa said. "It was enough to say that one person in a village was helping the partisans, and the brigades could burn every single house and shoot every last person living there. Think how much power that was to go to someone's head! Soon Abdul started believing he was some kind of local god, while the rest of us were plotting how to get rid of him.

"One morning my aunt sent Khatije to a nearby village, to an old Russian woman who could tell fortunes. She wanted to know what had happened to her son, who was at the Front. And Khatije thought she'd get her own fortune told, and see if Abdul was in it.

"That day changed Khatije's fortune all right. On that particular day the self-defence brigade had decided to clear the village, with its wealthy population of Russians and Greeks, and so they put about a whisper of collaboration... Only this time, someone really *was* helping the partisans. Khatije had just turned onto the main street, when suddenly there were bullets whistling about her ears, and roofs going up in flames, and partisans running silent as cats up the alleys."

"What did she do?" Ibrahim was so caught up in the story he hadn't noticed his coat smouldering from a stray spark.

Grandpa patted it out with his hand. "She dived for cover in the nearest house. Inside, crouched by the table, she found a terrified runt of a partisan who'd run out of bullets and didn't even have the wit to escape through the window when, with a bang, the door flew open and Abdul came in calling, 'Khatije! What are you doing in a collaborator's village?'

"My cousin plumped herself down on a stool by the table and smoothed her skirt tidily over her knees. 'I came to have my fortune told.'

"Abdul fairly dazzled in his new uniform. He prowled around the room, searching. 'There was a partisan in here.'

"Khatije looked as innocent as she could. 'I don't know where he went.'

"Abdul was still suspicious. 'I could have you shot, Khatije, for being here.'

"'Yes, Abdul. But you wouldn't, would you? Not before I tell you my fortune.'

"Well, of course Abdul was interested; he was so conceited. He sat down opposite her, resting his revolver in his lap and putting his hands in his bulging pockets, and said, 'Am I in it?'

"'Have you got something there for me, Abdul?' Khatije asked slyly.

"Abdul laughed and drew out from his pocket a blood-flecked handful of gold and silver. There were rings, and pocket watches, and a pair of earrings that Khatije recognized, because they were the ones that the Russian fortune-teller always wore in her ears.

"'I took them from a Russian,' Abdul said. 'And now they belong to the Tatars. That's how it should be. Would you like some earrings, my Khatije? If you pay me, of course.'

"Khatije slapped his hand off her knee. 'Don't you want to hear my fortune first?' she asked, leaning forward and staring into his dewy black eyes. 'It's a sad fortune, because the handsome young man who I love … dies.'

"'D-dies?'

"'That's right. He was a great hero of the Tatar people, but he was too good to live.'

"Abdul laughed and laughed. 'Are you trying to

110

scare me, Khatije? I've got no intention of dying.'

"'But you're no hero of the Tatar people.'

"Abdul became aware of a strange emptiness in his lap. He looked down and discovered that his gun had gone.

"'You're just a thief,' said my cousin Khatije. 'You sold your people for a pretty uniform and some scraps of gold. You aren't anywhere in my fortune.'

"Well, Abdul's dainty city manners went out of the window with the names he started calling her, until Khatije brought the gun down on his head and laid him out cold. Then she lifted up her skirt and said coolly to the little partisan who'd been hiding under it all this time, 'What are you waiting for? You can come out now, and wipe that cheeky grin off your face.'

"But that partisan just kept on smiling…"

"So *that's* how Khatije joined the partisans," Safi said. The flames of the bonfire crackled merrily, as though they were laughing. A few metres up the road, the police sat in their car and a second bonfire glowed, lit by a group of local men from Krasniy Mak. Safi wondered what they would make of this story, if they could have heard it. It was more complicated, but much better than anything she'd read

111

in the textbook at school. "Khatije was a hero, wasn't she?"

"She helped blow up bridges. She ambushed a whole German battalion outside Sevastopol. When she was caught, she never told the fascists anything, and they hanged her." Grandpa tossed another stick on the fire, and the bright sparks flew upwards. "It's all in the official records, if you know how to look. You have to know, because she's not called Khatije in the records; she's called scout Katya. You'd never know she was a Tatar. All the Crimean Tatar names have been changed to Russian ones."

"We'll rewrite the records," Ibrahim said, flourishing his pen as though he were ready to start right now.

Grandpa was looking at the second bonfire too, and the bored local men sitting around it. "In books about the partisans, there are lists of Russians, lists of Ukrainians, of Armenians, Greeks, Karaims ... and where the Crimean Tatars should be, there's a blank. A hole. A silence. What fills that hole is Abdul, Abdul, more and more Abduls, what the Russians would remember, so they can sleep easy in their beds."

11

IS THAT YOUR BROTHER?

The trouble started when Safi got off the bus in Krasniy Mak and Lutfi wasn't there. For the last few days she'd sat carefully still, wondering if Mama was watching the bus drive straight past their valley, and she'd thanked the driver politely when they arrived at the village. But today some of the other children didn't seem satisfied with that.

"Where are you going?"

"Home."

"You mean back to piss-poor Uzbekistan, where you belong?"

"I'm going to Adym-Chokrak. Please let me pass," Safi said calmly. Even if Lutfi hadn't been coming to meet her, she wouldn't have been too alarmed, because there weren't that many children, and several adults were walking close by.

"Oh, *Adim-Chakrak*," they mimicked, pronouncing it wrongly. "There's no place called that."

"Unless it's Tatar for squat."

"Tatar for pigsty."

"Tatar for hole in the ground that doesn't belong to you."

"Don't be so silly." Safi was determined not to be scared by a few children. She had police and unfriendly locals sitting practically on her doorstep half the time, after all. Several of the nearby adults had noticed what was going on, but they were just watching as if this was some kind of entertainment. Safi hitched her bag up on her shoulder and walked on. And then suddenly she stumbled and went flying, her bag falling off, her palms thudding painfully onto the chalky roadside. She actually thought she'd just fallen over a stone – how *stupid* – when a foot kicked her bag away and she realized someone had tripped her up.

"What did you do that for?" she said, pushing herself up on her knees and thinking that *now* would be a very good time for Lutfi to appear. "Give me my bag back."

"Yuck! We don't want it." The feet were kicking it around.

"It stinks."

"She stinks."

"It's got her dinner in it, oh, puke…"

"Boiled sheep's eyeballs…"

There were pounding footsteps, a thump, and Lutfi had arrived.

"Leave her alone, you little creeps."

That was only the beginning; Lutfi knew a lot of rude words. There were more thumps, and then he was off, chasing the children away up the road.

Safi inspected her palms miserably. There were sharp white stones embedded in them and they were starting to bleed. She began to gather together the things that had fallen out of her bag.

"There's this as well."

A girl was standing along the road, holding Safi's pencil case. Safi recognized her from the bus, but not from the crowd who'd surrounded her.

"It didn't get broken," she added encouragingly.

Safi wondered whether to take no notice or run away, but her hands hurt and she needed her pencil case. While she was deciding, the girl trotted up and held it out. "Here. You should ignore those morons.

I like your hair. Is that a Tatar style?"

Safi put a self-conscious hand to her several long red-brown plaits that Mama still helped her with, even though she was growing up now, and hoped they weren't too full of dust. "It's just mine."

"It suits you. Was that your brother? He's *gorgeous.*"

And then everything was just as Safi was used to. The girl was gazing dreamily after Lutfi, like girls always did. It was something about his curling reddish hair and green eyes; they couldn't resist him, not anywhere.

"You don't look like Tatars."

"What do you mean?"

The girl shrugged. "I dunno. I thought you'd be really dark, or have funny eyes, like Uzbeks or Arabs or something. What's your name? I'm Lena."

"Safi."

"Sophie?"

"No. It's short for Safinar."

"Safinar." The girl tried it out experimentally. "It's pretty. You should wash that grit off your hands. Want a toffee?"

"Thanks." Lena seemed harmless. In fact she seemed quite nice, and as familiar as the giggly

Uzbek and Russian girls who had hung around outside their house in Samarkand waiting for Lutfi to come out. She was a bit older than Safi, with freckles and feathery brown hair twisted up in a knot skewered with a pencil.

"Don't you want to see if he's all right, your brother? What's his name?"

"Lutfi. I'm sure he's all right."

As she spoke, Lutfi came back into sight. "Hey! Leave her alone."

"I'm helping," Lena said. "Did you get those idiots? They don't really mean anything; they've just got no brains and nothing better to do. Want to come to my place, and Safi can wash her hands? Are you Safi's brother? You look really similar."

You know he is, Safi thought crossly. And we don't look that alike, because no one goes around gazing after me, although perhaps, one day, when I'm fifteen… She hardly allowed herself to think.

Lena was playing with her hair, letting it fall loose, pegging it up again with the pencil. "Come on. It's just up here, and we've got some *zelyonka* for those cuts."

There was no one in at Lena's house. Lena dug out the green-dyed iodine from a cupboard, and

Lutfi dabbed it onto Safi's palms, doing the protective big brother act while Lena flirted about.

"So how come you're living out by Mangup-Kalye? Why didn't you buy a house in Krasniy Mak or Bakhchisaray?"

"No one wants to sell houses to Crimean Tatars," Lutfi said, glowering. "Haven't you heard? If we can't buy houses we can't get residence permits; if we can't get residence permits we can't go to school or get jobs; if we can't get jobs we're illegal; if we're illegal…"

"I get the picture. That's really unfair. Still, you could build a house nearer the village. I mean, there's not much out at Mangup-Kalye. Just a load of old ruins."

Even if no one else in Krasniy Mak wanted them, Safi thought Lena would be quite happy to have Lutfi as a neighbour. "It's where our grandfather's village was," she told her. "Adym-Chokrak. There were lots of houses, and a mosque, and our Grandpa lived his whole life there until he was seventeen."

"You'd never know," Lena said thoughtlessly. "Seems a bit weird, going back to something that's totally disappeared. Life's crap here anyway. My dad says Crimea's totally going to the dogs since perestroika. Don't know why you wanted to come back here really."

"Because it's home —" Safi started to say. But Lutfi interrupted her.

"That's because you're Russian, and the Russians have ruined Crimea. It doesn't mean anything to you. You're just occupiers; you don't know what home is."

"Actually I'm half Ukrainian," Lena returned coolly. "And my home's right here, thank you very much. Isn't it time you got out of it and went back to your amazing invisible village?"

Safi was furious. Lena might have been flirting annoyingly, but she was nice. After Lutfi had stomped out Safi lingered, feeling divided in loyalty.

"Thanks for the *zelyonka* and stuff."

"What's up with your flipping brother? *I* don't mind if you've come back. Makes life more interesting if you ask me."

"I don't know what's up with him," Safi said honestly.

"Oh well, *you're* all right anyway. See you on the bus tomorrow. Don't worry about the others; I'll look after you." Lena's expression was friendly and conspiratorial as she closed the door.

Safi trailed back to their valley behind Lutfi, who quickened his pace every time she tried to catch up until they were both almost running.

"Stop!" she called at last. "Please! I'm getting a stitch. I want to talk to you."

"I want to get away from that dump of a village," Lutfi growled. "I never even got to post my letter because of those scumbags."

"They aren't all like that. Lena's nice."

Lutfi just snorted contemptuously.

"Please don't tell Papa about today, Lutfi. I want to keep going to school."

That made her brother stop. He turned round to face her, a light in his green eyes. "What did you say?"

"I want to keep going to school. It isn't that bad." Safi wanted to joke about enjoying lessons, like Mama had, but she didn't recognize the look in Lutfi's eyes. "It's nice being with other kids, even if a few of them are idiots. There are some Tatar children there," she added, wheedlingly. "You're all so busy building the house, and it's so quiet. And Mama wants me to go…"

"You're unbelievable. You'd let Russian kids beat

120

you up, slag you off for being a Tatar. They stole our land from us and you'd let them treat you like that."

"They don't all treat me like that. Lena—"

"That patronizing cow?"

"She's not patronizing! Lutfi!" Safi could see that he was going to tell Papa, even though she couldn't believe it. And if that happened, the growing tension between their parents would blow up in yet another argument. Papa was already unhappy with Mama for insisting on the school; he thought she wasn't trying hard enough to build their home at Mangup-Kalye. Safi hated them quarrelling.

She looked at the fierce, angry light she'd never seen before in Lutfi's eyes. She and her brother had always been best friends. He'd told her his secrets, and she'd kept every one of them. "Lutfi. If you tell Papa about today, I'll tell about you and Larissa."

Lutfi's face went shocked. Then he turned his back on her. Safi couldn't catch up with him again all the way to the valley; but anyway, she wasn't sure she wanted to.

12

CRIMEAN SALT

"So here I am all on my own, one woman living with twenty-six men, and I didn't even know half of them beforehand! Oh, of course people are talking. The men are nothing but kind and respectful to me, though."

"But they don't know about Andrei."

"No, not yet…"

There was someone in the house with Mama, huddled by the stove warming her hands in the dim light of the paraffin lamp. She turned round as Safi dropped her school bag in the corner, holding out her arms with a big smile.

"Safi, *balam*! How's my favourite girl?"

"Zarema *Tata*?"

Safi returned the hug, astonished and delighted.

"The very same. Oh, I've missed you."

"I've missed you too."

Zarema had changed amazingly. Instead of the pretty, plump figure Safi remembered in its flowered frock, she was thin and gaunt, dressed like Mama in old trousers and coat. Her smooth, creamy coffee-coloured face was all hollows and cheekbones.

Zarema saw Safi's startled gaze and laughed wryly. "I know, you'd hardly recognize me, would you? I always did think I was a bit too fat; at least I can't complain about that any more."

It was wonderful to see her. Zarema and her husband, Remzi, had been close family friends in Samarkand. Zarema was several years younger than Mama, and to Safi she'd felt almost like a big sister. When she got married she'd had a proper, huge Crimean Tatar wedding, with a feast of whole roast sheep stuffed with rice and nuts, piles of *lyepushki* nearly reaching the roof, and dancing till dawn. Then two years ago she and Remzi had left with their baby, Ismet, for Crimea. Safi and Mama and a whole crowd of Tatar activists had waved them off at the station with promises to write and phone and meet again in the homeland before too long.

"We said the next time we'd see each other would be here in Crimea, didn't we?" Zarema seemed to read Safi's thoughts. "I didn't expect it to be quite like this, though, did you? I never thought I'd be all alone with Ismet, no house, no husband." Zarema's eyes were bright with unshed tears.

Mama glanced at Safi. It was the look that said, *Go into the other room; we've things to discuss.* Safi, bursting with questions, looked back crossly. Where was she supposed to go? The other rooms were dark and cold and full of building materials, while outside it was mistily damp.

After a moment, Mama sighed and patted the stool beside her. She rubbed Safi's cheek briefly when she sat down, before turning again to the Primus stove. It gave a pop and a blue flame shot up before vanishing with a hideous stink of paraffin. "Oh, curse the thing!" Mama exclaimed.

"Never mind, the water's hot enough."

"I'm sorry; there's no coffee, and we've run out of sugar," Mama said apologetically.

"And I've turned up empty-handed – what kind of a guest is that?"

"Don't be silly, Zarema."

Safi thought of the gleaming coffee pot and

grinder, still wrapped up snugly in the box in their cellar. In Samarkand the pot had been out on the table almost every day, because the house had always been full of guests: Safi's and Lutfi's friends, clever laughing women from Mama's work, Papa's comrades in the national movement, old Tatars reminiscing about Crimea with Grandpa. Coffee was the proper Tatar drink for guests, but now they couldn't afford it. And anyway, no one came to visit them.

Smoke poured out of the wood stove. The Primus stank; the lamp stank. The tea was lukewarm, and there were no sweets or biscuits to go with it. There was a sudden *tappety-tap* and all three of them jumped, automatically looking round for buckets and bowls and plastic sheeting. They'd forgotten that the kitchen finally had a roof of sorts. It wasn't the rain anyway; it was only the tap of nails where Mehmed was up a ladder working on the beams. He was shouting to Papa, working on the other side, "Lutfi needs to understand: violence is never the answer."

"We have to achieve this by peaceful means. We need Tatars in parliament!"

"Oh, parliament!" Zarema snorted with laughter.

"How things have changed! You, Elmira, running the Samarkand health department. Me, a city librarian. And look at us now. Do you remember learning at school about the Siege of Leningrad? How the Russians sat starving while the city was surrounded, no bread, no sugar, no light, burning their own furniture to keep warm? What do you think we're doing now? We burned Ismet's cot yesterday, the one Remzi made him. It's the Siege of Leningrad all over again!"

Mama began to laugh too. The smoke made their eyes water, and the joke made even Safi laugh, although she couldn't really see why it was funny, and anyone coming in would have thought they weren't laughing at all but crying.

"The blessed Siege of Leningrad." Zarema wiped her eyes. "I wasn't sorry to see the cot go. Ismet's too big for it now, and it made a fine blaze." She was twisting her wedding ring round and round on her finger. "I must listen out for the bus. Andrei'll sound the horn when he comes back to collect me. He asked me today if I was married. I told him ... I told him my husband was dead. Was that really wicked of me?"

Safi watched Mama all over again give her the look that meant, *Go into the other room*, and then remember she couldn't, and sigh resignedly. "I don't know, Zarema."

Zarema smiled crookedly at Safi. "My husband's gone back to Uzbekistan. He couldn't stand it here any longer: the waiting for land, the police, everyone hating us, no one giving him a job. And our money ran out. He went back and left me with Ismet."

"I'm sorry." Safi couldn't think of what else to say. She was shocked. Remzi had been a close ally of Papa's in the national movement. He was a singer, and had gone all round Uzbekistan collecting the old Tatar folk songs. He'd always talked about going home to Crimea, and had taken his family before Ismet was even a year old.

"Maybe it's for the best," Zarema said. "If he couldn't cope with the hardship, he's not the man I thought he was. But you're not to tell any of this to your father, Safi."

"All right." Safi bit back her questions.

"You're lucky with Asim, with your father. He wouldn't go running."

That was true, Safi was sure. But she wondered if Remzi and Zarema had argued before Remzi had left, the way her parents argued now. She felt very grown up sitting here with the two women complaining about menfolk, and she wasn't sure she liked it. Back in Uzbekistan she'd have chatted to them about clothes and friends and school, and then she would have run off with Jemile and left them to their women's talk.

Zarema was looking around the kitchen, at the buckets of water, the jumbled pans and packages of rice, pasta and flour. There were far fewer packages than when the container had arrived. "Do you remember my wedding, Elmira? We cooked for six hundred guests, and there was still so much left over we were feeding the homeless of Samarkand for a week afterwards. Now I'm cooking for twenty-six, and there aren't enough supplies for six. Twenty-six hungry men squatting on the land, and me! But what else was I supposed to do? Remzi went off and left me with four pegs and a piece of string marking my land, and not a brick to my name. So I'm cooking for the others, and when we finally get the permission they'll help me build my house. They're good to me."

"They're Crimean Tatars. And you're a hero of the Siege of Leningrad."

"That's what Andrei says too. He doesn't care about gossip."

"He might have to, soon. And you too, Zarema."

"I know." Round and round she twisted her wedding ring. "It's so hard here, alone. Did you think it was going to be so hard?"

"You could go back too," Safi suggested timidly.

The two women looked at her as if she had sprouted horns. "Go back?"

"To Uzbekistan. I mean, if Remzi's there." Safi felt herself going red under their stares.

"No I couldn't." Zarema sat up straight, and stopped twisting her ring. "This is where we belong. The gossip's nothing. Where else can I stand up and say, 'You can't question what I do, because here I have a right to be'? It's my land, it's my home, and there's nowhere else in the whole wide world for me but here."

Safi bowed her head humbly. The cheerful *toot toot!* of a horn sounded in the distance.

"There's Andrei." Zarema buttoned her coat and got up. "He's gone miles out of his way for me; these villages aren't on his route at all. I mustn't keep him waiting." She hugged Safi's mother tightly. "Things'll get better, won't they, Elmira?"

"Of course they will."

"You'll see, Safi."

Down by the road Refat and Ibrahim were sitting under a battered umbrella next to their notices. Refat was writing to his mother, and Ibrahim was annoying him by reading over his shoulder and suggesting amendments. Opposite, the police lounged under the hedge. Two tipsy-looking men from Krasniy Mak muttered dreary insults. Safi noticed they had captured one of the signs that said REBUILD OUR ANCIENT TATAR VILLAGE! Someone had crossed out BUILD and written above it BURY and added at the end in small letters AND THE TATARS TOO.

Refat chewed the end of his pen. "'I promise I'll go to Kermenchik soon, *Ana* dear, and see if your house is standing…'"

"No, Refat, you should write: 'I haven't forgotten about Kermenchik and your ancestral home. But you must understand, things have changed a lot in Crimea. I don't know when I'll have time…'"

"Doesn't matter – she'll still yell at me next time she writes," Refat said gloomily. Every single letter Refat received, along with urging him to get married, was a reminder that he should visit the village where his mother had grown up. Mehmed and Ibrahim tried to discourage him from going there, though; they said that even if it were still standing, her house would have been given to someone else.

A big blue and white bus rounded the corner and slowed, tooting again.

"Kermenchik is on Andrei's bus route," Zarema said. "He'll take you there for free. He's such a good man." She sighed wistfully. "The first time he saw me he said, 'I always felt there was something missing from Crimea. And then the Crimean Tatars began to come back, and I understood what it was. Crimea without Tatars is like soup without seasoning. That's what you Tatars are. Crimean salt.'"

The bus stopped. It was empty except for the driver, a small, fair, dainty man who climbed out to take Zarema's arm and escort her up the steps as if she were a princess. The locals wolf-whistled and shouted, "What is this, a private bus service for Tatar slags?"

Refat put down his letter and stood up abruptly, thin Ibrahim next to him barely reaching his shoulder.

"You should be ashamed of yourselves, speaking in front of a lady like that," the driver said quietly to the locals. He turned to the Tatars. "Anyone else want a ride?"

"Maybe to Kermenchik…"

"I don't think you should go, Refat," Ibrahim said, but Refat shook his cousin's hand from his arm.

"Well, let me know when you decide." The driver waved as he got back in the cabin. "If I can I'll come and pick you up."

"You're very kind to us Tatars," Mama said. Safi thought there was a strangely antagonistic note in her voice.

"Crimean salt!" he replied. "That's what you are – Crimean salt!" The door swung shut and the bus drove away.

"Is that Andrei?" Safi asked.

"That's Andrei."

"And he's Russian."

"That's right." Mama looked at her, stern and troubled. "Now Safi. Don't mention this to Papa."

"I won't." Safi wondered what her father would say about Zarema and Andrei. She guessed it wouldn't be anything very nice. "It's not fair," she remarked as they walked back to the house. "I couldn't even get a bus driver to stop for me on his main route, and Zarema's got one going right out of his way for her."

"Ah, well, when you're a bit older I'm sure you'll have all the bus drivers of Crimea falling at your feet," Mama teased. "Still, I hope this Andrei doesn't bring Zarema even more trouble than she's got already."

"Why would he?"

Mama frowned. "You know Tatars. We don't forgive betrayal." She looked at Safi's puzzled face. "Oh, never mind."

Papa and Mehmed were still banging in nails and shouting comments at each other across the roof, their hair flattened to their heads with damp. Lutfi and Grandpa sat in the *chaykhana*, sanding strips of wood for the window frames. Safi climbed in and leant against Grandpa, inhaling his dusty, comforting smell of pipe smoke and coffee. How could he still smell of coffee, when they hadn't drunk it for so long? He was like the pot and grinder out in the salt steppe, holding memories like coffee dust.

Grandpa looked down at her, his lined brown face folding into the smile he never gave anyone else. "Hello there. What's the matter?"

Safi knew she couldn't say anything to him about Zarema and Andrei. "Nothing. Tell me a story, *Khartbaba*. A proper old Tatar story."

13

THE DEBT

Grandpa stroked Safi's plaits gently. "Why don't you tell me a story instead, Safinar?"

Safi looked startled. "I couldn't do that," she said. "I don't know any."

One day it'll be you telling the stories, Grandpa thought. But he said, "*Bir zamanda bar eken, bir zamanda yok eken.* Do you know what that means? 'Sometime it was, or sometime it wasn't at all.' That's the proper way to start a story."

Grandpa leant back, trying to ease the ache in his chest. "When I was the same age as you, my mother told me tales of Alim, the last great horseback hero of Crimea. Even the mountains took pride in Alim, because in him dwelt the bravest folly, the deadliest

134

aim, the most pitiless scorn and the most indulgent heart. For seven years, all Crimea talked only of Alim the outlaw. This was many years ago, when my grandfather was a little boy, and suffering like all the rest under the heavy hand of the Russian tsar and his officials. Seven times Alim was captured, and seven times he escaped. The poor loved him, the rich feared him, and only one man sought a meeting with him. That was the old tsarist chief of Karasubazar. That man's glance was so keen you could not escape it, not even under the ground. Two dancers can't dance on one rope: that's what the wisest old Tatars said about Alim and the chief."

Lutfi stopped sanding and leant his chin on his hand, listening with alert, bright eyes.

"That was the year of the black frost in Crimea. The poor people endured it, but it was no easier for the rich, when the hoof beats of Alim the horseback bandit rang loud on the frost-hard roads. Alim was everywhere. He was even in the house of the chief of Karasubazar. He walked inside boldly and said, 'What reward will you give me if I betray Alim?'

"The chief didn't recognize him. He said, 'When I've Alim in my hands, I'll put a hundred roubles in yours.'

"And Alim laughed and said, 'Here was Alim in your hands, and still you couldn't hold him!' Then he jumped out of the window and rode away swifter than the wind.

"Alim rode to Kiziltash, where there was a cave to shelter him in winter. Only Batal from the village coffee house knew he was there, but Batal would sooner swallow his own tongue than betray Alim. Batal had a daughter, Shashne, and Alim loved and indulged the little girl. He sent her Turkish fezzes and embroidered slippers; he gave her gold earrings for her pretty ears."

"Lucky Shashne," Safi said wistfully. She wished a handsome hero would give her presents like that. She hadn't had anything nice and new for what felt like years.

Lutfi made an impatient noise. "Go on."

"Little Shashne boasted about her presents. She told her friend, a rich trader's daughter, 'When I'm grown up, I'm going to have Alim for a husband.' The trader heard it and he rode to Karasubazar, because he was afraid of Alim, and to be afraid means to hate.

"The chief came with his guards to Kiziltash. 'Not a hen leaves a henhouse, not a pigeon leaves a

windowsill of this village, until Alim is in my hands.'
Then the Crimean Tatars understood that it was the
end for Alim.

"That night a terrible storm broke the trees in the
orchards and howled over the mountain. In the
secret cave, Alim dreamt that circles of black snakes
hung from the roof. One reached down, slippery
and cool, and twined round his neck like the hang-
man's rope.

"Alim awoke, and there was a rope round his
neck. On his chest knelt the chief of Karasubazar,
and the chief said, 'You were in my house once as a
guest, Alim. Now, see, I've come to visit you.'

"The day they brought Alim in, Kiziltash was a
dead village. All the Tatars were trying to hide from
the keen gaze of the chief of Karasubazar; hide
under the ground they would, if they could. The
chief looked a question at Alim, and the outlaw
answered, 'I know. Now there'll be no more horseback heroes in Crimea.'

"Alim stood in shackles, and with him Batal from
the coffee house. Only Batal's little daughter,
Shashne, was there, crying, because she had no one
to look after her now.

"The chief said, 'I was almost forgetting, there's a

debt on me. Remember I told you, when I've Alim in my hands, a hundred roubles in yours. Now I have Alim, the money is in your hands.'

"Alim looked at Shashne. He said, 'Give it to her.'

"The column moved away down the long road, and now Alim has gone for ever from the mountains of Crimea."

There was a sudden sharp clatter. It was Lutfi, throwing his piece of wood down on the table. "They betrayed him! The Tatars themselves!"

"But it was the trader," Safi said. "Because he was rich. It wasn't Shashne's fault, not really."

Lutfi scrambled out of the *chaykhana*. "It's a stupid story." He walked away quickly towards the bonfires and the police.

Up on the ladder, Mehmed called something out, and Papa laughed. The nails going into the roof went *tappety-tap-tap*, like the sound of hoof beats, riding away down a distant mountain road.

14

HAVE YOU COME FOR
THE TREASURE?

Andrei threw the bus round the bends with the reckless joy of a bobsleigh rider. The other passengers seemed accustomed to this, but Refat's face was tinged green. "If I die on the way, write to Mother and tell her I did my best to get to Kermenchik," he said to Safi.

"You can't die; think what she'll say!"

"Oh, I know what she'll say. 'It's not enough that Allah saw fit to let the Russians invade Crimea in the first place, that He allowed that oaf Stalin to send us all away, that He gave me a stroke six months ago so I couldn't return to Crimea; no, He had to let my fool of a son take a lift with a kamikaze bus driver...'" Refat sighed gustily. "You're right,

Safi. We'll just have to hold on tight."

Refat had argued with Mehmed and Ibrahim and, a week later, finally taken up Andrei's offer to drive him to Kermenchik. In private, Mehmed had asked Safi and Grandpa to go too. "I don't think Refat realizes what it'll be like," he'd said worriedly. "I don't want him to be on his own."

The road looped down the valley between smooth high cliffs. In the flashes of sunlight the cliffs gleamed silver; in the shadows they were dark violet. Silver and purple clouds raced. At the head of the valley, Ai-Petri Mountain dazzled with its cap of snow.

Refat pointed. "Up in those cliffs are the caves where Alim the bandit hid out, and where my uncle when he was a boy kept an old rifle and took pot-shots at the Germans."

"Did he hit any?"

"Of course. They came after him in one of their jeeps but Mother stole the commandant's bicycle and rode through the woods to warn him. Then that lousy Hamzi Shustov, the son of the village head-man, told on my mother, because he was sweet on her but she didn't want anything to do with him, the cross-eyed slimy son of a – ahem…"

Safi giggled. Refat was the gentlest, sweetest-natured person she knew; he never had a bad word for anybody. "Refat, you don't even know him. How do you know he was slimy and cross-eyed?"

"How do you think?" Refat patted his pocket, bulging with his mother's letters. "She never did get a chance to pay him back for telling on her, and she'll never forget it until she does."

"Here you are!" Andrei called out, as the bus came to a crashing stop. "Schastlivoe. I'll be back this way in a couple of hours."

Schastlivoe, which meant "happy" in Russian, was what Kermenchik was called now. Safi jumped out, eager to see what a real Crimean Tatar village looked like. She was puzzled why Mehmed and Ibrahim had tried to persuade Refat not to come here; she thought he was lucky that his mother's village was still standing, unlike Adym-Chokrak.

Grandpa took Safi's hand and tucked it under his arm. Refat pulled out the fat packet of letters and began to read as they set off down the muddy, crooked lane. The new leaves on the trees shone bright as sudden flames in a flash of sun, and the banks were thick with violets. There was no one around but a few ambling dogs and a solitary, skinny black hen.

"'Next to Anife Batalova's, that miserable old witch – she still owes me a dozen eggs – make sure the fountain is still there, although it was never the same since that trollop Catherine the Great ordered another well to be dug further up the valley…'"

Safi giggled again. Refat's mother had no respect for anyone. In her letters she talked about Stalin, the Russian empress Catherine and even Allah in exactly the same way as she talked about her former neighbours.

The fountain was made of stone, with a graceful arch carved in the front and some lines of Arabic script. The trough was choked up with weeds and rubbish, but when Safi filled her hands from the pipe and drank, the water was deliciously, coldly sweet.

"'What does your mother say about the water?"

"'This one fountain had enough water for the whole village, even for that stuck-up schoolmaster's wife who collected twenty pails a day to wash herself and her husband, although why she bothered, Allah only knows: no amount of scrubbing would make the old skinflint smell better than a billy goat's backside –' Oh! I beg your pardon."

"Billy goat's backside yourself!" said a woman who had emerged from behind the fountain. She wore an old flowered housecoat, and she smelt distinctly goaty herself. "More Tatars, are you, come back to see your former homes?"

"Our homes," Grandpa corrected her.

"Well, I know what you're looking for," the woman said slyly. "Don't worry, I won't tell."

"What do you mean?"

"That's right, don't let on." The woman tapped her nose significantly. "Good luck with it." She disappeared again behind the fountain, but as they walked on Safi saw she was following them, although she pretended to be picking up firewood or kicking stones out of the road.

"Did your mother ever say anything about her?" Safi asked. The woman wasn't old enough to have lived here fifty years ago, but she seemed exactly like one of the old witches or misery guts or halfwits that, according to Refat's mother, had filled this village.

"Oh no, there were no Russians living here then…"

Anyone who didn't know him might think Refat was scary-looking, he was so big and black-haired, with round black eyes like a real Mongol Tatar, his ancestors from long, long ago. But Safi did know him, and she knew he was feeling sad. Like herself with Adym-Chokrak, Refat had grown up with stories about Kermenchik. The place was still lovely, folded snugly into the steep green valley, but it was falling down: a half-wild, crumbling tangle of a village. The long one- and two-storey Tatar houses, washed white or blue, looked as if no one had done any repairs on them for years. Dingy curtains hung in the windows; the muddy yards were full of abandoned furniture and tools and dogs and weeds. In one house a boy opened the door to watch them as they passed, and closed it again with a bang. The schoolhouse was full of goats; they stuck their heads out of the glassless windows, waggling their ears inquisitively. A man carrying a bucket stopped and stared, before scuttling away without even saying hello.

"Anife Batalova, the schoolmaster, Hamzi Shustov... They've all gone." Refat looked as if he was trying to wake from a bad dream. "They're all strangers here now."

"Is this what Adym-Chokrak looked like?" Safi said softly to Grandpa. She could see that the houses had once been pretty, with their wooden balconies and red pantiled roofs. They were approaching an especially nice one, with wooden pillars, painted sky blue, holding up the porch.

"Imagine it when people cared about it, and yes, this is what Adym-Chokrak looked like."

"This is Mother's house," Refat said.

They all stared at the rotting, peeling pillars, the sagging roof patched with rusty iron where the tiles had slipped. A child's plastic chair stood on the doorstep, and the balcony windows were full of red and pink geraniums flowering riotously behind the glass.

"Mother hates geraniums." Refat took a deep breath, strode up to the door and knocked on it loudly.

Silence.

"That woman's still following us," Safi whispered to Grandpa.

"Look, there's someone in the house," he whispered back.

Behind the dirty glass and the geraniums a pale face was looking out. As Refat knocked again another face appeared, and then ducked out of sight. No one answered.

Refat rattled the door handle. It was locked. Safi suddenly wondered how she'd feel if someone as huge and scary-looking as Refat came knocking on her door, if she knew she was living in a house that had been taken away from someone else. Perhaps she wouldn't answer either, not right away.

"Open up!" Refat bellowed. He turned aside and sat on the plastic chair. It was very small, so that when he sat his knees were near his ears. Carefully he put down next to him the pile of letters, with all their detailed descriptions of this beloved house where his mother had grown up. And then he began to cry.

Safi felt tears prickle her own eyes as the sobs rattled painfully through Refat's big body. She turned to Grandpa, aghast. "Maybe Mehmed and Ibrahim were right to tell him not to come back after all."

The door opened a crack and a little girl slipped out, closing it carefully behind her. She looked about six, just Lenara's age. Staring disapprovingly at Refat, she pushed a tiny handkerchief into his hand and placed next to him a very small teacup.

"Have you come for the treasure?" she said.

Refat couldn't reply. He mopped his face blindly with the handkerchief.

"What treasure?" Safi asked.

"The treasure you buried when you left here. You know, gold and old swords and … and … brooches an' stuff." The little girl stumped down the steps. She had a grubby face and a big gap where her front teeth should be, just like Lenara. "That's why you've come back to the house, isn't it?"

There was a rustling behind them. The woman from the fountain was pushing nearer through the bushes. When she saw Safi looking she stopped and began to pick her nose absently.

"If you tell us where it is and give us half, you can have the house back," the little girl announced. "That's what Pap says."

Safi looked up at Grandpa. There was a hard, fierce smile on his face that reminded her of Papa.

"Gold," he said to the little girl.

"Swords," she agreed.

"Brooches."

"An' stuff. That's right. Fifty-fifty."

"Behind the back wall," Grandpa said. "Four paces straight on. What's next, Safi?"

"Oh…" Safi wasn't sure if this was a joke or not. "Then five paces to the right, past the walnut tree."

"To the left."

"Wasn't it to the right?"

"To the left, and it was six paces."

The little girl frowned in concentration, mouthing the words after them.

"If you had invited him into his own house, perhaps Refat *Aga* would have told you exactly where it is," Grandpa said, and it wasn't any kind of joke any more. He put a hand on Refat's shoulder and helped him up. "We'll come back, and maybe we'll reach an agreement about his treasure. Or maybe we'll claim this house back for the people it rightly belongs to. You tell that to your father."

"Four paces straight an' six paces right. Four paces straight an' six paces right."

"Left," said Safi.

The little girl stuck out her tongue and ran back into the house. They heard her shouting, "Papa! Pap!"

Refat blew his nose into the tiny handkerchief. It looked as though it had come from a doll's wardrobe, and the plastic teacup from a doll's tea set. Safi picked up the bundle of letters and together with Grandpa guided Refat gently up the road again. The air smelt of violets and manure; the young leaves twinkled and then were extinguished as a silver cloud rushed overhead. When they were near the fountain again, they saw the woman hurrying back the way they had come. She had a spade over one shoulder.

"Can we really claim the house back?" Safi asked Refat hesitantly. "Is that what you want to write to your mother?"

It was the wrong question to ask. Refat's eyes filled again with furious tears.

"What can I write? They changed the name of her village; they called it Happy! Some idiot geranium-grower is occupying her house and letting it fall down and wouldn't even open the door to me. Squatters! They took this land and they ruined it; it'll never be the same. Look at them!"

On the flowery bank near the fountain, two men were lying curled up back to back, snoozing blissfully as babies. They were dirty and unshaven, in old ragged clothes. They snored softly, breathing out a miasma of onion and alcohol.

Refat raised a foot to kick them awake.

"Don't do that."

A man was coming down the road towards them. He had the lean, dark look some Tatars had, and a slight squint. "*Salaam aleikhum,*" he added. "Leave

149

them alone, friend. They're just like children who never learnt the first lessons about life. Who else would come here after the war, on promises of something for nothing? They got our land and our houses, and still they want something for nothing; now it's treasure or some such rubbish... Are you from Kermenchik?"

Refat nodded.

"So am I. My name's Eskender Shustov."

"*Shustov?*" Refat suddenly stood up straighter. "Tell me, Eskender Shustov, where is your kinsman Hamzi Shustov?"

"My father Hamzi died in exile, may his soul rest in peace." When Eskender Shustov frowned his squint became more noticeable.

Refat's face lit up with joy. Deliberately he clenched his fist and spat on it, and then he punched Eskender Shustov right in the jaw.

"Now I've got something to write to Mother!" he shouted, enclosing the other, staggering man in a huge bear hug and kissing him on both cheeks. "Finally Hamzi Shustov has been paid back for telling on her!"

15

KEYS

The bus was empty on the way back, which meant it lurched round the bends more sickeningly than ever. Safi wished she hadn't drunk the strange concoction Eskender Shustov had offered them, home-made out of ground chickpeas, chicory and dandelion roots. The taste had been very familiar to Grandpa. "Like in Uzbekistan in the first years of exile," he'd said. "We fooled ourselves into thinking it was coffee."

Eskender Shustov was living in the half of the schoolhouse that wasn't full of goats, along with several other Crimean Tatars whose families were from Kermenchik or nearby villages. It was a mouldy, dilapidated building, far worse than the unfinished house at Adym-Chokrak.

When he heard the whole story, Eskender's loyalty to the Crimean Tatars won out over any grudge he might have felt for the bruise rising on his jaw. "There are Russians living in my father's house too," he told Refat. "And they'll never give it back, even though I've got the deeds." He pulled a bundle of yellowed papers out of his pocket and threw it on the table. "For fifty years my father and then I kept the papers to our house with us at all times, so we were ready to come home. When I came back, even the lock on my house door was the same. This table here was my father's. I found it in a farmyard; the Russians were using it to chop feed for the pigs."

Pigs! There was a hiss of indrawn breath, tongues clicking with outrage. Pork was forbidden for Muslims.

"They might as well have renamed this village Porkers," Eskender said bitterly.

"Porkers," Refat muttered now, staring out of the window at the wooded hillsides flashing by. "Schastlivoe. Why did they rename my village Happy?" He was clasping the seat in front of him so hard, his knuckles were white. Safi couldn't believe that just a couple of hours ago she had thought him lucky that his village was still standing. She could see now that funny, gentle Refat was gripped by a hard baulked rage that reminded her of the anger she saw sometimes in Lutfi.

"I'll tell you how they changed the place names," Grandpa said. "Stalin ordered it just a few months after the Tatars were deported. He wanted to remove every last trace of us from Crimea. The order went to the Soviet newspaper *Red Crimea*, and it arrived at night-time, when the only person there was the secretary. An order from Stalin himself couldn't be delayed, of course; the maps had to be redrawn. The secretary had two books lying on his desk: a gardening manual and a report on the Soviet liberation of Crimea. He was in a panic, and he just crossed out all the old place names and wrote over them words out of those books. Apricot, Almond, Red Poppy. Red Guard and Partisan."

"And Happy?" Refat demanded. "How did he choose that name for a village where women and children and old men— where *my mother* was dragged from her home and sent away to live or die as best she could?"

"Perhaps it was the last one, and he was glad to be finished," Grandpa said. "Perhaps that secretary had a sense of humour…"

"Russian humour!" Refat snarled.

Safi looked at the driver's cabin, where Andrei was swinging the great steering wheel of the bus. Andrei had been kind to them and Zarema. She found herself hoping he couldn't hear what they were saying about his people.

Refat was feeling in his pocket. He took out two keys, and showed one of them to Grandpa. "Look. This is the key to my mother's house."

Safi stared at it wonderingly. It was made of brass, as shiny as if it was used every day. But this key hadn't opened a door for nearly fifty years.

"I'm like Eskender Shustov with his papers," Refat said. "My mother carried this with her every single day of her exile, until she gave it to me to bring home. All of us Tatars, we all have keys. And those keys have names: Kermenchik, Akmesjit, Ozenbash, Haja-Sala. All the Tatar towns and villages that you'll never find now on the map."

"In my pocket I carry the key to a house," Grandpa said slowly. It sounded like the beginning of a story, but although Safi looked at him expectantly, he did not continue. Grandpa's hand was in his pocket, cupped gently around the familiar shape there, tracing the rounded end like a heart, the sharp flanges that sooner or later wore holes in the lining of every pocket he'd ever had. I've carried this key since I was seventeen years old, Grandpa thought. And it is completely useless. The lock it was made to open no longer exists.

"Now what shall I do with it?" Refat said angrily. "They might as well go in a museum, all of them. Locked up in a glass case, labelled THE KEYS TO OUR PAST."

"And this one?"

The second key in Refat's hand was a modern one with a plastic grip. As Safi reached out, Refat closed his fist over it suddenly.

"It's the key to my house." He looked at Grandpa and Safi defiantly. "In Uzbekistan. I might need it again. You can't live with pigs. At least in Uzbekistan I had a fine house, a vegetable garden. My neighbours were Uzbeks, good Muslims."

"But Refat, you're not really going back, are you?" Even as she asked, Safi wondered where her key to their Samarkand house was. She could picture it vividly; it had been tied to a piece of coloured string so she could hang it around her neck. But the door had hardly ever been locked, because friends

155

and neighbours were always passing in and out, calling to Mama or waving newspaper articles and protest leaflets at Papa. Remembering all that warm liveliness made Safi want to cry. If Refat went back, their valley in Crimea would be quieter and lonelier than ever. She swallowed hard and said, "But what will your mother say?"

And this time it was the right question. "You're right, Safi. She'll say, 'It's not enough that my good-for-nothing son is still a bachelor and won't give his old mother any grandchildren; no, he even disregards my other great wish to come back to Crimea. What did I do for Allah to punish me so in my old age?'" Refat smiled ruefully. "No, Safi, I'm staying here. I'm too scared to go back and face that. I might as well give up both these keys to the museum."

"Good." Yet as well as reassured, Safi felt a tiny bit disappointed. Refat's words were like another nail in the lid shutting down on her memories of Samarkand, a key locking them away in the past rather than keeping them alive as a place to return to. Confused, she hid her face in Grandpa's sleeve. "Are we nearly back at Adym-Chokrak? I feel a bit sick."

Grandpa's thoughts were far away. Deep in his pocket, he turned over his own sharp, heart-shaped key with his fingers. He thought, No. I don't want to give it up, not yet.

Papa was waiting for them at the side of the road. Andrei opened the bus doors and said pleasantly, "Here they are; I brought them back safe and sound," but Papa completely disregarded him. He took Safi's arm and pulled her off the bus, past Mehmed sitting by the bonfire and up round the pond.

"Let me know if you want a lift anywhere else," Andrei called, but no one took any notice of him except the locals from Krasniy Mak, who shouted, "Another bloody collaborator. You should be ashamed of yourself." After a moment, the bus doors closed and Andrei drove away.

"Papa." Safi would have liked to have said thank you for the ride. "Papa, he only took us to Kermenchik."

"Oh yes. Another kind-hearted Russian bus driver." Papa stopped and swung Safi round to face him. "Your mother told me you knew the difference between truth and lies. But you've been lying to me."

"But... What?" Safi's lips began to tremble. She couldn't remember the last time her father had looked at her with such anger. As if she'd betrayed him. "What do you mean, Papa?"

"That school bus driver. You told me you were getting off at Krasniy Mak because one of the children there was helping you with your homework. But that's not true, is it? The driver refuses to stop for you here, and Lutfi has been meeting you in Krasniy Mak because otherwise the children bully you. That's the truth, isn't it?"

The vile, bitter taste of the ersatz coffee they'd drunk in Kermenchik suddenly filled Safi's mouth. She looked aside, and there was Lutfi walking quickly away from them, around the other side of the pond. He must have told, after all. She'd guarded his secrets for him, and now her brother had told on her.

"You all kept it from me," Papa said. "My own family, and you lied to me so that you could get out of working on this house I'm trying to build for you. This house that you don't believe in, none of you. Do you even care how far we've got? Do you even realize there's no money left and I don't know how we're going to finish it? You were too busy elsewhere. My own family, and all you want is to forget who you are—"

"Papa, it wasn't like that."

As well as rage, there was a kind of dreadful hurt in Papa's face. He suddenly flung Safi's arm away so violently that she stumbled and almost fell.

"It wasn't—"

Papa took no notice. He started back down towards the road, where Grandpa and Refat were still standing, bewildered.

"Asim," Grandpa said sharply. "Where are you going?"

"To have it out with that school bus driver, where do you think?" Papa pushed past rudely.

Mehmed stood up by the bonfire. "Come back, Asim. Don't be a fool; you know you'll only make things worse." He and Refat hurried after Papa.

Safi watched in shocked dismay as the three men walked towards Krasniy Mak, gesticulating and arguing, their voices echoing even after they had turned the corner out of sight.

16

SAFI'S HOUSE

The eye or the graves. The graves or the eye. Safi stood at the junction where the path met the main track. She couldn't decide which was worse. While she was agonizing, her feet seemed to turn of their own accord to take her back past the spring to the building site, the *chaykhana* and her family.

"No!" she said out loud. She turned, put her head down and plunged up the path to the right before she had time to hesitate further.

The leaves on the trees were bigger now, forming a canopy of the brightest, softest transparent green for the birds to bask in. When she picked off a leaf, it was cool and silky-downy between her fingers. All sorts of new plants had appeared around the moss-padded rocks: budded spires pushing up between spotty leaves; fat, fleshy red stems. While the Crimean Tatars were struggling to build down below, up here things were busy growing, effortless and unchallenged. They didn't have to make a life for themselves out of sweat and tears and bricks and plaster. Life just happened to them here on this mountain, on Mangup-Kalye, and no one minded, no one told them they had no right to it. It would be nice to be a plant. You just put down roots and got on with growing and flowering and having seeds and then dying again until next year.

"Safinar…"

Was someone calling her? It sounded a little like Grandpa's voice, a long way away. She stopped for a moment to listen. But Grandpa never came up here. It was just a trick to make her stop. No one was following her; no one knew where she was.

Safi wasn't sure whether she was exploring or running away. She had discovered how Papa had found out about the school bus and the children. It wasn't from Lutfi after all; it was, stupidly enough, from Lena. Ibrahim had been in Krasniy Mak buying nails, when Lena had walked past and recognized that he was Tatar, and she had cheerfully told him how she was looking after Safi so no one bullied her. She was no doubt hoping that word of it would get back to Lutfi, but it got to Papa instead.

Halfway to Krasniy Mak, Mehmed had persuaded Papa to turn back without picking a fight with the school bus driver, but now it seemed that her father's thwarted anger was being turned on his family instead. It was impossible to tell him that Lena was nice, that the other kids didn't bother her any more, and that there were Tatar children in her class. He was so furious he was hardly speaking to Mama. And Lutfi was not speaking to Safi at all.

There were enough problems already with Krasniy Mak. The police were by the pond every day, blocking the road so that there was a confrontation every time Mehmed wanted to use the car. More and more local men, often drunk, came to stand around jeering and shouting. Lutfi, spoiling for a fight, had been banned by Papa from going anywhere near them. Just before the news about the school had reached Papa, the police had brought an official letter from the village council. It informed them that the land they were on was part of a designated historical site, and that they were squatting illegally and "might be removed by force."

Mama had tried so hard not to have an I-told-you-so look, it was almost funny. Ibrahim and Grandpa had drafted a reply saying that their case was being reviewed in Bakhchisaray, and that if anyone had rights to a historical site it was the Tatars, since a Crimean Tatar village had historically stood there. Since then, nothing more had happened.

"Who cares about it anyway?" Lena had said dismissively. "No one here's interested in history or anything. They're only writing letters because the tourist season's starting soon, and they're worried about losing business."

Despite Lena's irritating flirting with Lutfi, Safi missed her a lot. She missed Ayshe from her class too, and Rustem, who, she had a sneaking, delicious suspicion, rather liked her. It was so unspeakably unfair that as soon as she had made new friends she had lost them again. Without school, there was no one to talk to and nowhere to go. Papa would not let her walk to Krasniy Mak. Bakhchisaray was too far away. There was only Mangup-Kalye.

Something was rustling loudly among the plants

sprouting from the litter of last year's leaves. Safi stopped at once, her feet again turning despite herself to take her back down the path. With an effort, she stood still and peered into the gloom. A bright yellow-rimmed eye looked back. It was a blackbird, pausing to study her from one eye and then the other before returning to its rummaging. Then it flew up to the top of a gravestone, reeled off a faultless flourish of song, and darted into the trees.

She had happened on the cemetery before she realized it. There were no ivy tendrils laid over the path today, and she wondered who had removed them. The back of her neck prickled.

The narrow path wound between the mossy, higgledy-piggledy tombstones. They were just stones, after all, and they belonged to the Karaims, a people so old no one knew where they came from or remembered their names. But there were ghosts here, Safi knew, in the half-light, and they didn't want her to go further.

Back in Samarkand she had gone everywhere. All day long she'd roamed with her friends, sometimes taking Lenara along to play in the market with its fat silk-clad women selling spices and pomegranates; in the park; along the alleys between the blue-tiled mausoleums of Shakhi-Zinda. She'd been at home everywhere. Here she was scared even to walk round a bend in the track. Crimea was nothing like she had been promised. Instead of opening out into the home of Grandpa's stories, her world had shrunk to four damp half-built walls, a narrow green valley, the muddy track to the spring. And she hated it.

Safi forced herself to follow the path. Further on, she came to the dank ruins of what might, long ago, have been houses. They reminded her unpleasantly of their own little house down in the valley. Trees and bushes sprouted from gaping dark holes in the walls, and a cold, musty smell breathed out of them. She thought she heard more rustling inside and rushed past, her heart beating fast. If this was the city Refat had talked about, it was horrible.

She was supposed to be exploring with Lutfi, but as soon as they were out of sight of the house he had stomped off somewhere without a word. Safi had been glad that he had not given her away about school, but since she had accused him about it, his self-righteous fury with her was almost worse. Sometimes she thought she hardly recognized her careless, good-natured brother in the angry person he'd become.

Go back, whispered the ghosts. If she'd been with Jemile or looking after Lenara, she might have enjoyed the spookiness of this path. They'd have made up stories about monsters and bandits and the hero Alim to scare themselves. On her own, it was just awful. But she'd set off to get to the top of Mangup-Kalye, and she couldn't turn back now.

The path got narrower and muddier, and because she was hurrying she slipped and fell. She lay looking at the mud on her clothes, almost crying. Why had she started this? She must be a long way away by now, and no one knew where she was. If only Lutfi had come with her. If only she'd never left her family behind.

Down below, Mama and Papa would be arriving at Bakhchisaray around now. Mama would be hurrying to the post office to call Uzbekistan and talk to Lenara. Papa would be meeting up with his friends and carefully working out the cost of supplies and building materials. The house at Mangup was turning out to be more expensive than anyone had expected, and because of changes in the government, prices were soaring. Papa and Mehmed had constantly gloomy faces now. There was nothing to eat but the cheapest pasta and bread, and the building work had almost stopped.

Safi realized why the path was muddy: ahead of her was a spring bubbling up and overflowing a deep stone basin. She got to her feet and plunged her hands, then her hot face into the water. It was startlingly cold and a shiver went right through her, starting from the top of her head and running out of the tips of her toes. After it had gone she suddenly noticed the silence settling around her. The water chuckled tinily, dwarfed by the utter stillness of the woods. Not even the birds sang.

She hurried on, legs aching, and her panting breath was the only sound in the world. The climb seemed endless. The path got narrower and narrower, the trees closing her in and filtering the daylight to a green darkness. She couldn't remember where she was going or why. She wished she'd never come.

And then quite suddenly she emerged into another world.

The trees gave way and there was space: huge, airy, bright. The top of the plateau was covered with a fine carpet of silver-green grass, scattered with starry white flowers as thickly as a fall of hail.

A fresh breeze sighed over it with a gentle, tireless, lonely sound.

Safi filled her lungs with it. At the edge of the plateau the wooded slopes plunged down dark and steep, but she stood above them looking out into air. Such distances! Such a falling away of valley after valley after valley, abrupt hills and ridges receding in ever softer shades of blue. A lake gleamed amidst thick gauzy forest like a mirror, and right in the furthest distance, where the palest blue of the mountains turned into the pale grey of the sky, a line glittered.

She had come up between the first and second knuckles of Mangup-Kalye, and now something took her hand and led her onto the back of the fist into a strange, high green country, dotted with ruins and pocked with caves. The white flowers bounced up again from under her shoes. There were tiny irises, and funny blue flowers like bunches of grapes on fine stalks, and some kind of herb that smelt sweet and fresh and heady. She met a cow, thoughtfully pulling up the grass with its huge rough tongue. The caves were hollowed out of the edges of the plateau, connected to each other by worn staircases cut into the rock. Some had windows, and doors opening onto a sheer drop of a hundred metres down to the woods below. Once they had been houses and churches, wine cellars and mosques and kenessas, but no one had lived in this city for hundreds of years. They had left it full only of wind and light. She found one cave with precise round hollows and troughs cut into the floor, and another that had a square pool of water. She clambered and burrowed and scrambled among them happily, but still something led her on and further on, until she found the best cave of all.

She easily might have missed it, because the entrance was from one of the smaller caves, through a hole tucked away in a corner of the floor. No one very fat or tall would have been able to fit through it. But when Safi dropped down into the cave below she caught her breath in delight.

It was almost perfectly round, with a ceiling domed like an egg and a single pillar holding it up. Curling around one side was a broad stone seat, and above it a series of arched alcoves cut into the wall. Another part of the wall was open in a window, with a ledge to stop you from falling. Outside the window lay Crimea, all its soft colours shading away into the sky.

It was the most complete small room. Its smooth silvery stone was wind-scoured and spotlessly clean, and the roundness made it cosy. The little niches in the wall were just the right shape for keeping a few things in. The stone seat was gently scooped out as if generations of people had sat there making it comfortable before leaving it for Safi.

Sitting back on the seat, Safi realized she felt completely happy. She felt at home. She wasn't even thinking how much she'd like to show this to Jemile or Lenara. No one else had been up here: not Mama, not Papa, not Lutfi, and Grandpa never even talked about it. This was *her* place.

How could she ever have been scared of Mangup-Kalye, when this was at the top? She knew that this was where she'd come always.

"It's my house," she said to herself. And then, softly, out loud, "Safi's house."

17

THE OTHER SIDE OF THE ROCK

"Safinar!"

Grandpa called again, but he didn't really think she would hear. She'd gone ahead up the path long ago without seeing him, and he couldn't run to catch up, not any more. His breath caught and wheezed painfully in a chest worn out with years of labour, years of grief. I'm too old, Grandpa thought. And what did I want to say to her anyway? She'll look her questions at me that I no longer know how to answer.

Grandpa sat down on a rock to rest. The trouble with being old is that children think you know everything, he thought. They look up with trusting faces; my Safi looks up, drinking in my stories, expecting me to have all the answers because I'm beyond puzzlement, beyond doubt, beyond fear. And then these children grow up a little more, and now they think – Lutfi thinks – that I know nothing worth knowing because I'm beyond love, beyond joy, beyond pain. Sometimes they're right; mostly they're wrong. But it's a wrongness we can do nothing about; it's just the way life is. There's a rock bigger than Mangup-Kalye between the old man I am and the children they are.

Grandpa folded his arms over his aching chest to keep it warm. The birds sang. The new leaves smelt fresh and sweet. His head in its round sheepskin cap nodded gently onto his chest.

I was on their side of the rock once, on the path that leads to the top of Mangup-Kalye, just about bursting with joy and love and fear. When I was a boy, I could run up that path in fifteen minutes. A bomb might fall on our heads any second, a plane tumble and crash; there were partisans hiding in the forest like Alim's bandits; and my Safinar was waiting for me. Eh, life was worth living!

I'm on the path up Mangup-Kalye now, but I'm on the other side of the rock. I don't know how long it would take me to climb to the plateau; just the thought makes my old legs shake. But more than my legs, it's my heart that's trembling. So much in Crimea has changed. So much has gone for ever. I'm scared to go up this path, in case, in case —

"*Khartbaba?*"

Grandpa jerked awake. Safi was standing in front of him, watching him anxiously.

"Are you all right?"

"I'm a silly old man," Grandpa said. "When I was a boy running up this path, old Gulnara *Tata* would look round from the Karaim gravestones, her hands full of moss and ivy, and call out to me, 'What's the hurry, silly boy? Don't you know, nothing changes on Mangup-Kalye? Run any faster and you'll catch up with your own future!' Those words always sent a shiver down my spine, I didn't know why."

Safi considered. "What a funny thing to say." She hoped Grandpa wouldn't ask her where she'd been, but at the same time she was curious. This was perhaps the first time he'd mentioned Mangup-Kalye in his stories about when he was a boy. "Why did you used to run up the path?"

Grandpa stood up stiffly. "I'm cold. And we should be getting back to the house."

Safi hesitated. The house was where her family

was, and going back meant returning to the arguments. She wanted to hold on to the clean uncomplicated happiness of the caves a little longer, and hear a story about them that was as clean and simple. "Won't you tell me first? Please?"

Grandpa looked into Safi's trusting face gazing up at him. He sat down with a sigh, drawing her to lean against his knee. "From the top of Mangup-Kalye we could see the whole war in Crimea. The Germans had an army base up there, as they knew you could see so much. But they never saw as much as we did, because they were invaders; it was not their land."

Grandpa took his pipe out of his pocket, looked at it, and then put it back again. "From the top of Mangup we could see the bloom of red and black where the anti-tank missiles landed, and then minutes afterwards the boom of the explosion would reach our ears. We could see the racing sheets of orange that was the forest burning. Best of all, we could watch the aeroplanes. They zoomed below us along the valleys, the Soviet planes with red stars on their wing tips, the fascists with black crosses. Down in the village, we knew our mothers and grandmothers were hiding with cushions over their heads, muttering prayers from the Koran. From up here we could look down on the heads of the pilots and gunners; if we were fast enough, we thought we could lean out and spit and they would look up, shaking their fists and swearing ... but we were never quick enough."

"It sounds fun," Safi said. She'd never imagined before that war might be fun.

"Yes. The only pity was that by 1944 we had no one left to cheer for. The Soviets had already gone and left us once to the German occupiers. Now the Germans were on the retreat; and anyway, we no longer believed their promises. All we cheered now was the brightest explosion as another plane, red-starred or black-crossed, went down in flames.

"One morning a Soviet plane was shot down ... about here. Yes, it must have been where we're sitting right now." Grandpa looked around, as if searching for a sign of that long-ago crash, but there was nothing but the spring leaves gently fingering the air. "We saw the pilot's parachute pop open to hang like a fat mushroom. And then his plane blew up, and the blast tore his parachute in half and tossed him all the way down into Ali Memetov's grapevines.

"The Germans picked him out of the vines, and brought him to our house. He had two broken legs and a mouthful of smashed teeth. They brought a small sack of semolina too, and I was more interested in that, because we hadn't had enough food for months. But the semolina was for the pilot. The Germans told us to look after him; they said that if anything happened to him, we'd be in trouble."

"Why did they bring him to you?" Safi asked.

"They knew he wouldn't die in my mother's care. When one of the Germans billeted in our house was shot by the partisans, she nursed him back to health. The Germans didn't know it, but she had looked after a wounded Red Army soldier cut off in the retreat in 1941, and sick partisans from the forest. Like us watching the air fights from Mangup, my mother didn't care whether it was red stars or black crosses. I didn't care because, Soviet or fascist, they were as bad as each other. But my mother believed they were as good as each other; they were people who were suffering and who needed kindness."

"You mean my great-grandmother," said Safi. "Who married Seit Ahmet when he thought he was too old." She remembered that when Grandpa had told them Seit Ahmet's story, he had promised another one about kindness. Perhaps this was it. "Go on."

"My mother fed that Soviet pilot semolina gruel through a straw, and the Germans measured how much the sack went down and how much the pilot recovered, as if they had an exact formula for correlating the two. I never found out why he was so important to them. He wasn't much older than me. After a few days he stopped dying and sat up bright-eyed and miserable and jumping at every noise. I thought he was listening for the partisans, but I don't know whether he hoped they would rescue him or knew they would shoot him.

"When the sack was empty, the Germans came and took him away in an army lorry as if he were a sack himself, as though all that semolina had just been transferred from one container to another. My mother cried when they took him away."

Grandpa leant forward. "But I didn't care. This was not our war. The Germans made us promises so they could use us against the Soviets, and when the Soviets came back they used those promises to get rid of us for good. I understood that even then. There was no one to stand for the Crimean Tatars except ourselves. When the Red Army took back

Crimea, they came to our village and asked who had handed over that pilot to the Germans. They didn't ask who had saved his life by feeding him gruel, by caring for him. We Tatars stood together and shrugged our shoulders. We did not know. We did not remember. No one in the village pointed a finger at my mother, and because of it Ali Memetov and my Uncle Murat were shot in front of us. The week after, they came and took us all away."

Safi looked down. She was confused by this story. It wasn't at all funny, and she wasn't entirely sure if it was sad either. "So was your mother wrong to look after that pilot?"

"What do you think?"

"I don't know."

Grandpa said, "My mother never lost her faith in kindness. My war was the war for the Crimean Tatars, for our homeland, and I've fought it all my life since I was seventeen years old and they took me away from it. Your father's fighting it now, Safi. And your brother. My mother's was a different war. A war for kindness, and she too fought it all her life. When she cared for that German soldier and that Soviet pilot, she was hoping that somebody somewhere was doing the same for my cousin Khatije with the partisans. She hoped the same when I was beaten by the camp guards on the Hungry Steppe, and when my son, Asim, your father, was arrested and sent to prison in Uzbekistan. She's dead now, but I know she hasn't given up the fight."

"Why?"

"Because in my heart I have the same hope for you. In the end, Safi, kindness is all we've got."

"You mean like Andrei was kind?" Safi scuffed the ground with her shoe. "Papa doesn't like him because he's Russian; he'll never like Lena either. I thought maybe you didn't as well."

Grandpa had said Papa was fighting a war for the Crimean Tatars. Was that the same war she was fighting, and Mama? Safi didn't know. She was used to assuming her parents were right (except about not allowing her to go to the cinema with Jemile on Saturday afternoons, or get her ears pierced, or let Lutfi go out with Larissa). She'd never questioned the big things they'd told her all her life: that she was Crimean Tatar and her home was here in Crimea, and the most important thing she could ever do was return to claim it. Now she simply wasn't sure any more. How could Crimea be her true home when she knew nothing and no one here, when people like Lena and Andrei had lived here all their lives? She wished Grandpa had told her a different story, one that was easier to understand and that cheered her up.

Grandpa stood up, wincing at the stiffness in his bones, and held out his hand to her. "Come along. Time to go back." He knew exactly what she was thinking, as he looked at his granddaughter's dissatisfied face. He wanted to tell her that she was growing up. But that was something Safi had to realize for herself.

You're growing out of my stories and into your own, he thought. For all these years we Crimean Tatars have made our home in the past, in stories and memories. All the years fighting to return to Crimea were like steps up this path onto Mangup-Kalye, fraught with danger and excitement and fear, and at the end of it the promise of where we belong, just like as a boy I was running to my Safinar waiting for me. But at the end too is the future, where I don't belong. Too much has changed; I'm on the wrong side of the rock. The future is the children's.

18

HAVE YOU EVER SEEN THE SEA?

A week later, everything changed. Promptly on 1 May the sky turned high clear blue, the sun shone and the May day holiday brought tourists to the ruins. A few turned up at the pea-green pond in cars; more often they came walking, loaded with rucksacks and sleeping bags and guitars and water bottles. They were young, cheerful Ukrainians and Russians from Kiev or Moscow, and they were surprised to find the signs by the pond, the Tatar house and tents. Some of them turned back, or got in their cars and drove away. But others came on up the valley, and even more than their surprise was their pleasure at being able to buy cheap good food, and lounge drinking tea in Mama's shady *chaykhana*.

Now it was Papa who tried not very hard to hide his I-told-you-so look as he quickly put up another *chaykhana*. Mehmed drove to Bakhchisaray with the last of their money to buy ingredients and borrow every single Uzbek teapot and drinking bowl he could lay his hands on. Lutfi trekked up and down to the spring for water, Mama and Safi chopped onions and rolled pastry, while Ibrahim and Grandpa took turns frying *chebureki*. Refat took charge of the big pots of *plov*; he turned out to be a wonderful cook.

"If only I'd known that these last two months!" Mama teased him. "Just wait till all the girls find out. They'll be queuing up for you!"

The money from the visitors trickled in steadily. But along with the tourists came more locals from Krasniy Mak. They put down cloths by the pond and laid out bottles of lemonade, home-made wine, bread and cakes to sell. That way they got to the arriving tourists first. Then Papa put up a new notice by the road. It was bigger than any of their protest signs and said: TATAR HOME COOKING: CHEBUREKI, PLOV, UZBEK SPECIALITIES, TEA, with an arrow pointing up the valley. More visitors started to bypass the Krasniy Mak sellers. After a

182

day the notice disappeared and Lutfi found it floating face down in the pond.

"I told you they were worried about losing business," Lena said. She'd come over to the valley too, not to sell anything but to hang around the visitors ("It's so *boring* in Krasniy Mak; thank goodness for tourists") and to see Safi, although Safi thought that trying to get Lutfi to talk to her was also a pretty big reason.

"We've got more right to be here than they have; this was our village." Lutfi scowled at her. "Anyway, it's their fault if they haven't set up a proper business. It was up to us to start selling hot food and tea; Tatars have always been better organized and that's why you're scared of us."

"You can see their point, though," Lena said reasonably. "I mean, I know Adym-Chokrak was your village, but Krasniy Mak is our village and we've got to make a living too; and you did come along without asking and just set up here."

"We have asked! My father's been asking the pigging authorities for eight months to give us back *our* land, where we lived in *our* houses—"

"Don't bite my head off! Honestly, Lutfi, you've got a chip on your shoulder the size of

Mangup-Kalye. How would you feel if some Karaim or someone turned up and said they'd lived here before you and so it was their place and you had no right here at all?"

"Why would they do that?" Lutfi grinned suddenly. "They're all buried in that haunted graveyard."

"It's not haunted."

"Yes, it is. Only Tatars are brave enough to live near it; you Russians are too scared."

"Yeah, right…" Lena threw a handful of daisies at him.

The sunshine had brought all sorts of new flowers out of the grass. Now the house and *chaykhana* stood in the middle of the prettiest, floweriest meadow, sprinkled with white petals from the blossoming fruit trees. The leaves of the forest on Mangup-Kalye shone and sparkled as they tossed in the breeze, and the ridges at the top gleamed sharp and silver. Safi often went round the bend in the track now to look at the eye in the rock. With the sky through it, it was the unforgettable blue of the tiles on old Muslim mosques in Samarkand. She watched the tourists walking up the track with anxious envy. She hoped none of them found *her* cave, her house.

At least with their great rucksacks and guitars they'd be much too big to fit through the entrance.

"Hey, Safi." Lena tapped her shoulder. "Have you ever seen the sea?"

"Only from the plane."

"Well, my dad's driving to Alupka in a couple of days to see my cousins who are here on holiday. If you want you can come too and we'll go to the sea. What do you think?"

The sea... Safi remembered that ruffled carpet she'd seen from the aeroplane. "Oh, I'd love to. But I don't know if my parents will let me."

"Why not? It's just for a day."

Safi couldn't explain. Lena wouldn't understand that it was because she was Russian; she'd get all offended again. "We're so busy here," she said instead. "And they don't like me going off on my own."

"Lutfi can come too," Lena said immediately. "Ooh, I'll tell you what. There's an old Russian man living next door to my cousins who speaks Tatar." She regarded Safi with the triumph of a magician who has just pulled a rabbit out of a hat. "Really. He's ancient, and he's always talking about what it was like when the Tatars lived here. You can meet him, and then we'll go to the sea. There."

"I can't speak Tatar. Neither can Lutfi."

"Then bring your Grandpa along," Lena said, with a wave of her hand.

As they drove away from their valley two days later, past Krasniy Mak and further than she'd ever been in this direction, Safi felt her spirits lift. She sat beside the window in the back, with Lena next to her and then Lutfi. They went past sunny vineyards, the vines just starting to cover the lines of stretched wire, and then they turned onto a main road and before long there was the sea far below, a glorious silken expanse of blue. Lutfi wound down his window to let in the breeze, filling the car with the scents of salt and pine.

"It smells fantastic!"

"It's ozone," Lena said wisely. "Really good for you. The Russians invented it and brought it to Crimea."

"Oh, don't start that again!"

But Lutfi laughed and pinched Lena. She pinched him back. With every minute they left Mangup-Kalye behind, Lutfi seemed to get happier and less interested in putting Lena down. He was almost his old careless self, and it struck Safi how he must hate the valley as much as she did. Lutfi had never gone to school at all in Crimea, never had a chance to make new friends. He was always stuck with the men, building. Poor Lutfi didn't even know about the cave on the plateau that she escaped to as often as she could. She thought she would tell him about it, when she got a chance.

Now she leant forward and put her hands on Grandpa's shoulders. Despite Papa's good mood, now that they had money again and could buy materials to continue building, he'd frowned when Safi had told him about Lena's invitation. Then Grandpa had decided to come to meet the Russian neighbour who could speak Tatar, and there had been no more discussion after that. Safi secretly thought that the real reason Grandpa had insisted was not because he wanted to meet the old man, but because he knew how much she wanted to see the sea.

"Thank you, *Khartbaba*," she whispered in his ear.

Grandpa reached up and patted her hand. "We should thank Igor Petrovich."

"Don't mention it. Always glad of the company." Lena's father took both hands off the wheel to wave their thanks away. "Whoops!" The car swerved across the road and he corrected it hastily. He was brown and freckled like Lena, but much fatter. "So how long is it since you were last in Alupka?"

"Nearly fifty years," Grandpa answered in a hollow voice.

"Such a long time. I expect you'll find it's changed a lot. It used to be a wonderful place, when the Communists kept it in order. Everything was affordable; everything was organized. We all had regular holidays; there were none of the shortages we've got now, the power cuts, the unemployment. These last years since perestroika, Alupka's gone to seed, like the whole of Crimea. Like the whole damn country."

"Blah blah blah," Lena muttered under her breath.

"It's because of perestroika that we could return to Crimea," Lutfi said argumentatively from the back seat.

"Blah blah blah." Lena rolled her eyes.

"Do you still have any friends or relatives in Alupka?"

"They have all gone," Grandpa said in the same hollow voice. "Almost fifty years ago my father's brother lived in a house by the park. He was exiled to Kazakhstan."

"Honestly, Papa, you're asking really stupid questions," Lena said, hitting him lightly on the head. "You know all the Tatars were deported, so how could anyone still be there? Use your brain for once."

Safi was rather fascinated; she would never dream of behaving like this with her own father, and she wondered naughtily whether this was one of those "Russian morals" Papa was so opposed to. Lena's father at any rate appeared used to such treatment.

"That's right, that's right," he said meekly. He didn't seem to know quite what to make of his passengers; Safi kept catching his eyes in the mirror dubiously studying her and Lutfi sitting on either side of his daughter. "Well, you'll love talking to Arkady Yakubovich. Amazing old fellow, memory like a book; he can jabber away in that language of yours, but since his wife died he's got no one to speak it with. He lives next to the park too, by the way."

He didn't just live next to the park. He lived in the pretty pink-painted house where Grandpa's uncle had lived.

Grandpa was almost speechless. He got out of

the car and stared, muttering, "It's the same. The same…"

From one doorway a bundle of people as fat and freckled as Igor tumbled out, laughing and shouting. From another a very old man emerged. He looked disapprovingly at his noisy neighbours, and then he saw Grandpa beside the car, staring at the house. Very slowly, his face split into an astonished smile. *"Salaam aleikhum,"* he said. *"Khosh sefa keldiniz!"*

They left the two old men together, talking happily in Tatar over tea and biscuits, and went with Lena's cousins down to the sea. Alupka was full of roses, falling from lamp posts and over walls in extravagant cascades. Safi had almost stopped believing in the Crimea of her grandfather's stories, but the roses were as drowsily sweet-smelling as he had always described them. The little painted, peeling houses of the town were so jumbled together they looked as if they were about to slide into the sea below, but the cats on the windowsills and balconies lounged and stretched unconcerned.

"This bit of the coast has a microclimate; that's why the roses are out already," Lena told them.

"The sea'll be too cold to swim in, though."

Safi didn't think so; she was used to the jade-green, hurrying rivers of Uzbekistan that stayed cold as mountain snow even in the heat of summer. She told Lena about them as they took off their shoes and paddled out into the unbelievably blue sea and climbed onto the rocks. The water slapped and splashed noisily around the rock edges, but the weed growing on them underwater swayed silently and smoothly in green glass, as if listening to a different, dreamy rhythm. Hundreds of tiny red and brown crabs scampered sideways into the cracks, and then as the children sat still, soaking up warmth like the sun-warmed stone, they crept out again. Lena's cousins pounced and caught them, waving them in Lena's face so that she shrieked at the sharp pincers snapping almost on her nose.

Her cousins were three boys, the youngest as small as Lenara, the eldest a year or so younger than Lutfi. When Safi unpacked the lunch Mama had given them and carefully divided it up to share, they looked at it in disgust.

"What's that?"

"It smells weird."

"Like dog food."

"And that looks like a dog turd."

Safi looked down at the slices of *kobete* and the *churchkhela* in bewilderment. Mama had baked the pie specially, disregarding the expense of the meat, and the lumpy, sausage-like *churchkhela* were treats all the way from Uzbekistan. After weeks of living on not enough pasta and rice, this was a feast. "All right, don't eat it then. See if I care."

"You don't know what you're missing." Lena picked up a *churchkhela*. "You're so unadventurous. I'd like to see what you'd do if someone dropped you in the middle of Uzbekistan. Run off screaming if you saw a camel." She bit off the end gingerly. "It is a bit weird."

"Are there camels in Uzbekistan?" The youngest boy gazed at Safi.

"In the desert. You see them in town sometimes. They dribble."

"Camel turd…" The middle boy poked at another *churchkhela* disdainfully. Actually, Safi had to admit, it did look quite turdish.

"How did you know? Most people don't guess what it is, because it doesn't taste half as bad as you'd expect. People only eat it in really hot countries; the desert nomads use it for long journeys because it stops you sweating and keeps you hydrated."

Lena stopped mid-chew. "You don't mean…"

"It's only from very young camels that are still drinking milk, so it's quite rare and really expensive. It takes ages to dry – about five weeks – but it keeps a long time."

Lena had her mouth half open, with a look on her face as if she didn't know whether to choke or be sick.

"You're kidding! That's *disgusting*," said the middle boy.

"When you're trekking across the desert, one of those will keep you going for three days," Safi added helpfully.

"Wow," said the youngest boy, staring at Safi in total wonder.

"Present!" said Lutfi. He had crept up behind Lena, and now he dropped a scrabbling crab into her lap. Lena jumped and screamed. The crab scuttled away. Lena gulped and coughed a little. Then she put her hand to her throat.

"Oh no," she whispered. "I swallowed it. I just swallowed it. Oh no."

Lutfi gazed at her in puzzlement. "What's the matter?"

"Go on, tell us, what are those really made of?" The eldest boy pointed at the remaining reddish sausages.

"*Churchkhela?*" Lutfi looked at Lena's horrified face, and at the boys' wonder and disgust. "Oh, those. Yeah. It is a bit revolting, I suppose. But the crap is brilliant for dehydration; it's got all these mineral salts in, so doctors really recommend it for hot weather. It's from these birds in the desert in Uzbekistan, a bit like condors. There's a whole tribe of women who live in the desert and all they do is collect up the bird crap—"

"You *pigs*!" Lena shrieked. "I believed you; I really thought … oh, I was nearly sick!"

Safi rolled on the ground laughing. The youngest boy picked up a *churchkhela* and waved it at Lena, crowing, "Camel turd, camel turd."

Lutfi looked around with an absolutely innocent face. "What? What's the matter? It's actually really interesting. Anthropologists have studied this tribe of women and concluded that it's the only one in the world whose migratory patterns are totally dictated by – by p-p-poo…"

"Pigs," Lena moaned, hiding her face in Lutfi's shoulder and pummelling him weakly with her fists.

Lutfi patted her back soothingly. "That's right, let it digest; you won't have to drink again for a week now."

"Yeah, well, I wouldn't be surprised if you really did eat turds."

Lutfi looked up sharply at this, but the eldest boy had already turned his back and was wandering away, kicking up the pebbles.

On the way back from the shore, Lena put her lips close to Safi's ear and whispered, "Your brother is s-o-o-o gorgeous. It doesn't matter that he's Tatar, does it?"

"What do you mean?"

"Well…" Lena was twisting a lock of hair round her fingers. "You know. You're Muslims and all. You know people say you must be mafia or something, to have enough money to build your own houses. They say you want to start a civil war here, kick all us Russians and Ukrainians out and have laws like in Arab countries. Don't women have to cover their heads or faces all the time? And the men have loads of wives."

"Don't be so stupid," Safi said. "You've seen my

mother. She doesn't cover her face, does she? And she's Papa's only wife. We haven't got lots of money. I don't know anything about Arab laws, and the whole point of the Tatar movement is that it's peaceful." She suddenly felt deeply miserable. "Anyway, it isn't like you're marrying Lutfi; what do you care about how many wives people have or where we get our money from?"

"Yeah, but you're my friends," Lena said. "Aren't you?" She looked at Safi through the strands of hair. "So, what are those church things *really* made of?"

The sun was warm again, and Safi's skin smelt magically of the salt sea. "Not telling you. You'll have to marry a Tatar to find out."

19

YOU NEVER SAY SORRY

Arkady Yakubovich spoke Tatar better than Grandpa. The inside of the room overlooking the park in Alupka was full of cheap, modern Soviet furniture and knick-knacks, but as they talked in the language of fifty years ago Grandpa felt as though he were sitting in his uncle's cluttered workroom once more, surrounded by jeweller's tools and velvet pouches of semi-precious stones, sniffing the smells of hot metal and coffee warming over the Bunsen burner, watching his uncle tease out the coils of wire with tiny pliers held in his blackened silversmith's fingers.

"I'm Russian and my wife was Greek, but we were both born in Alupka and we always spoke

Tatar together; she never liked Russian," Arkady Yakubovich said. "Remember how we all spoke Tatar here, before the war? Few spoke it as beautifully as your uncle, though; he was a real scholar." His sunken, pale blue eyes creased up in thought. "Everyone in Alupka knew him and his filigree jewellery. We thought he was writing a great ethnic history of Crimea in his spare time. That's why the Soviets didn't like him, but they left him alone because he had silver in his pockets, and the chief of the propaganda department enjoyed talking to him."

"He was one of the only educated Tatars left in Crimea," Grandpa said. "The purges in the thirties, the war, even the German occupation, somehow passed him by."

"Well, the Germans were very polite, very educated. They had their own theories about ethnic origins, and the German commissar liked to discuss them with your uncle."

"He was no collaborator!" Grandpa exclaimed.

"Did I say he was?" Grimacing, Arkady Yakubovich bit into a dry biscuit. "Many of us were disappointed in the Soviets, and believed German promises. I still remember the gingerbread the fascists gave the children. No Communist ever gave children such gingerbread. If we all had to answer for what we did during the occupation, perhaps most of us would hang from the lamp posts, Ismail *Aga*."

It was soothing yet troubling to hear the honorific *aga* from a Russian man speaking Tatar, Grandpa thought. When he was last in this house he'd been no "older brother" to be respected, but a boy of seventeen, cadging a curl of silver for the girl he wanted to marry.

"Your uncle didn't believe it when they came to take him away," Arkady Yakubovich went on. "I remember when the soldiers arrived at his door in 1944, he just sat there like a fool saying it had to be a mistake. That's why he took nothing with him. No silver, no precious stones."

"If he had taken them, perhaps he would have survived in exile."

They sat in silence for a while, two old men remembering the past. Then the Russian said, "Crimea was never the same after you Tatars left. The people who came to settle here afterwards were scum. Riff-raff. All they knew how to plant was potatoes. They dug up the orchards, filled up the springs and the seashore with concrete and rubbish.

Like my neighbours. Good-natured enough, but idiots."

"Yet they gave you this house."

"More tea, Ismail *Aga*?"

Oh, these Russians, thought Grandpa. What I wouldn't give for a proper cup of coffee. His fingers trembled with anger as he took up his teacup. But he was an old man; it was undignified to get angry. It was ridiculous.

"What's that you said?" Arkady Yakubovich enquired.

"The Soviets gave you this house."

"Your house," Papa said. They were sitting in Mama's candlelit *chaykhana*, surrounded by the cool, starry May night. Mama and Papa and the men were recovering from a hard day working with the tourists, and Grandpa was telling them about his visit to Alupka. "That was Seit Ahmet's youngest brother's house, wasn't it? And he had no children, so it belongs to you now."

"Yes," Grandpa agreed. "That's what I told him. I said, 'My uncle died in exile, dreaming of the homeland, while you lived here in peace. By right this house belongs to my family, and you are still living in it.' I said to him, 'None of you, not one, has ever even said you are sorry.'"

"And what did he do?" Refat asked eagerly. Safi was sure he was thinking of his mother's house.

Grandpa smiled faintly. "He asked me if I remembered the cow."

There was a pause, and the hoot of an owl sounded down the valley like a plaintive question.

"Did you say, the cow?" Refat asked incredulously.

"No, *he* said, the cow." Grandpa stroked Safi's cheek where she rested against his arm, half asleep after her sun-filled, sea-filled day. "He told me about the people who lived in that house before my uncle. They were a wealthy Karaim family of landowners, with their own herd of cows. Then in the 1930s the Communists began collectivization, taking all land and livestock away from individuals and putting them instead into the Soviet collective farms.

"It was a crime to be wealthy, in the thirties. That family was stripped of everything it owned. The father was shot as an enemy of the people. All his cattle were collectivized, but there was one cow that didn't agree with the concept of common property.

She broke out of the collective farm barn and came stalking back to that house by the park, and the new owner had a hard job persuading the Communists he hadn't stolen her. The next day she was back again, mooing for her dead master. It didn't matter where they put her, behind what fences and walls, she always broke through." Grandpa looked around at the listening faces. "Arkady Yakubovich told me how that cow woke my uncle every morning, mooing under his window at five o'clock sharp. I don't remember it. I never asked how my uncle got that house. He got it nice and cheap, stolen from its owner. Something for nothing."

Papa rubbed the edge of the table moodily. "It's not the same."

"So many wrongs have been done in Crimea," Ibrahim said. "Decades of them. Centuries. I don't know if we can put them all right."

"What did you say to what's-his-name, Arkady thingy, after that?" Safi asked drowsily.

"I felt like a fool with my anger. A silly seventeen-year-old fool. Arkady Yakubovich asked me who should be saying sorry now, and I said that if we all had to pay for what we did, perhaps there wouldn't be enough lamp posts in Crimea."

"Lamp posts?"

Grandpa pulled Safi gently upright. "And then he went to get more tea. That's all. I think it's time you went to bed."

That wasn't really all that had been said. When Arkady Yakubovich had come back with the fresh tea, he was carrying a roll of cloth. "I told you your uncle took nothing with him when he left. Nearly everything of value disappeared afterwards, of course, to fund our great Communist Party via a few private pockets, but a few things I managed to save."

He unrolled the cloth. It was spotted with age now, but Grandpa recognized it immediately. Inside was the length of fine cotton he had once chosen so carefully, embroidered with the old Crimean Tatar patterns of the tree of life, the elegantly curved *nar*. And lapped in its folds was a small heap of tarnished metal. Grandpa untangled a pair of earrings like filigree stars, and a ring and bracelet linked with delicate silver webbing: a precious glove to adorn the hand of a Tatar bride.

It's easy but terrible to cry when you're seventeen; easier when you're nearly seventy. That was what Grandpa thought, the rheumy tears of old age filling his eyes as he handled the jewellery made by his uncle. Years ago, when I was seventeen, I brought this cloth to him, the *bogcha* in which to wrap my betrothal gifts. Here is the *marama*, the embroidered scarf I bought for my bride. And a spiral of silver for Safinar, that's what I begged from Uncle. I never dreamt of *this*…

"I think they are yours," Arkady Yakubovich said. "My wife wore the earrings a few times. You can give them to your granddaughter. This is my way of saying sorry; I hope you won't now evict an old man from his house."

"Of course not." But Grandpa could not bring himself to say thank you.

20

SURGUN

This was the day for true stories. It was 18 May, and the sun rose bright and blithe as if it had no heart. A day for picnics, for paddling in the sea, for lying in the grass beneath the knee-high daisies. There were small silken scarlet poppies on Mangup-Kalye now, and peonies smelling of warm sweet cakes. The caves were round suntraps; the valleys were lush with green and silver bird-full forest falling mile after mile to that line of light that was the sea.

It was a Crimean day that stood on tiptoe and shouted, *Look how wonderful I am!* It was the day for remembering how the Tatars had to leave all this behind.

As the chartered bus swung into the station on the outskirts of Simferopol, the morning sun shone right into Safi's face, dazzling her into seeing black shapes. She put her hands over her eyes. When she looked again, there were hundreds more shapes. The bus station was full of Crimean Tatars, standing quiet and purposeful, ignoring the police cars parked all around them. Pale blue banners marked with the Crimean Tatar *tamga* shifted gently over their heads, and a very low, wailing hum rose into the morning.

Bus after bus pulled into the station, bringing Tatars from Bakhchisaray and other villages and squatters' camps east of Simferopol. Safi saw a face she knew: Ayshe, her friend from school. She waved, and Ayshe came to join her. It didn't seem quite right to smile and laugh on this day, but they were delighted to see each other.

"I've missed you at school," Ayshe said. "Rustem's always asking about you."

"He is not." Safi flushed with pleased embarrassment.

"He is. We heard about the police at Mangup."

"There are lots of locals too, from Krasniy Mak and the other villages. They won't let the tourists come near us; they tell them we're bandits and thieves. They tear up our notices and they bashed Lutfi the other day when he tried to stop them." She didn't tell Ayshe how Lutfi had raged when Papa and Mehmed had pulled him out of the scuffle without letting him fight. Lutfi had called Papa a coward, and Papa had hit him.

"Why don't the police do something?"

"They just sit in the hedge and watch. If they interfere at all, it's to tell tourists that any business with the Tatars is illegal. And they won't let Mehmed drive in if he's got building stuff in the car."

"Maybe they'll get bored with it and go away," Ayshe suggested optimistically.

The sun was high when at last the Tatars formed into a column and moved off. Along the road into Simferopol locals stopped to stare, and curtains twitched in the windows as though anxious inhabitants were watching from the safety of their homes. At other houses, doors opened and more Tatars came out to join the march.

Ayshe waved at a group of people emerging from a gate. "That's my aunt's family."

Most of the family joined the column, leaving behind an old man who watched the Tatars filling the road with an indifferent gaze.

"Isn't their grandfather coming?" Safi was surprised. Everyone was there who could be, but today was really the old people's day. Her own grandfather was walking along steadily behind her, and everyone around greeted him with respect. "There are lots of cars if he can't walk."

"Oh, he's not their grandfather. He came with the house."

"What do you mean?"

"They bought the house with him in it. His daughter didn't want to look after him any more, so she sold the house on the condition that her father could still live there. Not that she actually cares about him one bit. She's gone back to Russia and never even telephones or writes. My cousins have to look after the old man. But you know how hard it is for Tatars to buy houses; they took the first chance there was."

Safi stared at the old man. "Is that true?" The way Ayshe recounted it so carelessly reminded her of the way Lena had said about the Tatars: *I thought you'd be really dark, or have funny eyes, like Uzbeks or Arabs or something;* and *People say you must be mafia.*

Ayshe shrugged. "What can you expect? I heard that another Russian family left their daughter behind when they sold their house. She was only about six, and really ill, and then she died and her parents just came back for the funeral and scoffed all the food."

"That's a terrible story. I don't believe it."

"Fine." Ayshe sniffed and took a deliberate step away.

Safi looked round at her own parents. Mama had a steadying hand on Grandpa's arm and they were talking together, but Papa saw her and his hard, fierce face softened a little, as if he'd seen something in her expression that worried him. She wondered if he too was thinking about Lenara, whom they'd left behind without even a house in Samarkand, and about how Mama hurried to the post office to phone whenever she could. The sooner they finished their new house at Mangup-Kalye, the sooner Lenara could come and join them.

Safi smiled at Papa, glad he was there with Mama and Grandpa and Lutfi. This was the day for terrible stories, for remembering all the things the Tatars had left behind, and what they had lost on the way.

They walked until noon. The traffic had to stop for them, and some drivers got out of their cars and shouted insults, even threw stones. It didn't matter. The pale blue flags fluttered proudly over the swelling crowd, and everyone, no matter how poorly they were living, had dressed in their best clothes. They chanted "Our land! Our rights! Our home!" They sang the old Tatar songs. And all the time the low, wailing hum rose into the dazzling Crimean sky, the hum of stories being retold. Everyone had tears on their cheeks, not just the old people. Safi had not been born at the time of the *Surgun*, the deportation into exile. Her mother and father had not been born. But that meant nothing. She wiped her eyes along with the others because these stories belonged to all of them. This was what it meant to be Crimean Tatar. You weren't one person; you were part of a nation, sharing a history, an identity, a family. The many stories blended into one story, the voices into one voice.

The eighteenth of May 1944. The soldiers came before dawn, to every town and every village throughout the whole of Crimea where Tatars lived. The fighting was over; there were no partisans and Germans to fear now, only the Soviet liberators. They banged on the doors and ordered us sleepy Tatars outside, with fifteen minutes to get ready and no word of where we were going, only that the Soviet authorities decreed that we be sent away for ever for treason to our country. They packed us into lorries and jeeps, then loaded us onto the trains like cattle. They took us away, and on the journey they let us die. No water, no air, no food in those railway trucks, only suffering. At one stop my mother ran for water, and she was late coming back. She reached out to climb into the truck, but through the closing doors I saw a soldier strike her hands away with a bayonet, and I felt her fall under the moving wheels. They came for my baby. I told them he was sleeping, but they said he was dead. They tore him out of my arms, and before he could scream they had tossed him from the truck. They killed my brother. He was told to dig the hole right there by the railway line where they threw the dead and the dying all jumbled together, no name, no marker. My brother refused, and they split his head with a spade and pushed him in with all the others.

Safi wept and wept. They all did. But they kept their heads up, and the Crimean sun dried the tears on their faces. There was only one thought in all of their heads. We Tatars have lived through this. We have waited and struggled for almost fifty years.

And we have come back. Nothing can stand against us, now we have returned to reclaim our homeland.

Simferopol's central square could hardly contain all the Crimean Tatars who had marched from every corner of the peninsula. Safi looked around, and all the faces were the same, salty with grief but hard and fierce and proud and determined. She knew her own face looked like that too, because it was how she felt. No wonder the Russians and Ukrainians, staring in huddles behind the ranked police, were frightened that the Tatars had come to take Crimea away from them. She understood now how Lutfi had felt after that last meeting he'd been to. He was standing with a group of boys and young men she didn't know, but when she caught his eye she knew her eyes were shining just like his. Safi lifted her head and sang along with the thousands.

> *"I've pledged to banish darkness from my land*
> *with light.*
> *How long can brothers be kept apart?*
> *If I, who promised light, don't catch fire and burn*
> *May my tears become a great sea of blood from*
> *my heart."*

A pure, clear voice joined the singing beside her. Safi looked round and saw that it was Zarema. She was wearing a dress today, one of her old flowered ones. It hung loosely from her bony shoulders. Next to her stood Andrei, carrying her son, Ismet.

"I never knew you were so many," Andrei said. "So many..."

It was strange seeing him standing there with the Tatars, when all the Russians were behind police lines, staring at them with fear and dislike. Was it thus they had stood and watched the trains in 1944 that took the Tatars away? Had they been like the drivers on the way here, shouting and throwing stones? The police at Mangup with their stupid disdain and hate, the school bus driver who had refused to stop for her and said their village did not exist? And suddenly Safi was angry with Andrei for being there, and with Zarema for bringing him.

The crowd pressed close and Andrei put his free arm round Zarema's waist to hold her steady. Safi realized that Papa and Grandpa were looking at Andrei too, at his open, marvelling face and his arms round Zarema and her son, and at the wedding ring still on Zarema's finger.

"When is your husband coming back, Zarema?" Papa asked in a cold voice.

Ismet leant his head on Andrei's shoulder, gazing at them with big dark eyes.

Grandpa said sternly, "That's a fine son you have. A real Crimean Tatar, blood and bone. He'll grow up to love his people and his homeland, not the Russians."

He could have said this in Tatar, which Zarema spoke well. But he didn't; he said it in Russian. The fierce pride faded out of Zarema's face. Andrei didn't get angry; he looked a little puzzled.

"I'm sorry," he said. "I'm sorry for what happened, but it isn't my fault; I wasn't even born then."

Grandpa and Papa turned away from him. Before she turned her back too, Safi saw Andrei's arm drop from Zarema's waist.

"I've pledged to lay down my life for my homeland.
What's death to me, if I can't dry my nation's tears?
What's life to me, even a thousand years as khan
When one day the grave will gape for me here?"

Safi's lips tasted of salt. At first it reminded her of Grandpa's story about the Hungry Steppe. *I am the ghost who will never let you go. We Crimean Tatars never give up, not even if you kill us!* Then it made her think of Andrei driving the bus away and calling to them. *Crimean salt! That's what you are — Crimean salt!*

21

MUST I REMEMBER THIS?

After the meeting many people went back to the camp in Bakhchisaray, to reminisce and gossip and be sociable: things the Tatars did best. There were great bonfires, and queues of people around the enormous steaming cauldrons of *plov* and *lagman* like the ones that stood on the street corners in Samarkand.

Safi sat quietly by one of the bonfires. After a day so immersed in collective memories and emotions that she'd hardly been able to remember her own name, she felt she was gradually coming back to herself, to her small head brimming with the thoughts and ideas of twelve-year-old Safinar Ismailova. The busy darkness, full of sparks from the fires, the hum of voices and the good smells of food, brought back that delighted alarm she remembered from when she'd first arrived in Crimea. The camp had changed since then. Now there were many houses in varying stages of completion, surrounded by buckets and planks and stacks of those familiar yellow building blocks.

But Safi thought that she had changed more than the camp had. She recognized the feeling of half-scared delight, but it seemed to have happened to someone quite different. Back on that first night in March, when Papa had taken her hand and walked with her down the row of shelters, she'd thought she was arriving in the world of Grandpa's tales. She had expected roses and sunshine, mosques and *medresses*, bandits and soldiers: a whole brightly coloured storybook Crimea. It was less than three months ago, but it felt like three years. The Safi she was then felt like a very little girl to the Safi she was now.

"What's going on inside that head of yours?" Refat asked, handing her a big bowl of *lagman*, thick with meat, vegetables and noodles. "You looked miles away."

"I was," Safi said. Of course, she was back in

exactly the same place she'd started from those few months ago, but it might as well have been, almost, a different planet.

"And you, Ismail *Aga*?" Refat's voice was respectful as he gave Grandpa his soup. "This day must bring back many memories."

The flickering firelight accentuated all the lines on Grandpa's face, and suddenly to Safi he looked like an old, old man. Inside his head were all the stories that had made her feel homey once, that had thrilled and delighted and scared and comforted her. It looked far too fragile to hold so much.

As if he had heard her thoughts, Grandpa said, "They burn, these memories. The screams of the dying, the casual cruelty, the hatred – sometimes I would like to open up my head and take them all out. Must they stay engraved on my heart for ever?"

After a moment, Refat said, "My mother always says there is nowhere else for the Tatars to live. She'll shout and complain, 'What is Allah thinking, making me remember things like this? Haven't I suffered enough? I lost my parents and sisters; I've buried six husbands – don't I deserve some peace?' But she's always known we would only find peace when we found our homeland again."

"*Six* husbands?" Safi asked, distracted. "I thought you said she celebrated her fiftieth wedding anniversary?"

"You try telling my mother you have to be married to the *same* husband for fifty years to have a golden wedding," Refat replied, so resignedly that everyone laughed.

"Perhaps she's right, though. I mean..." Safi paused, trying to sort out her thoughts. "The main thing is that she was married for fifty years, and not who to. It's like us. The main thing is who we are, not where we are. We've been Crimean Tatars all these fifty years in Uzbekistan or wherever." She stopped, startled. She hadn't really intended to say this aloud, and she wasn't sure if it was exactly what she meant anyway.

To judge by the silence, no one else was too sure either.

"That's wrong," Lutfi said at last, with a kind of violent stubbornness. "The Russians have got Russia to live in. The Ukrainians have got Ukraine. We can't be Crimean Tatars if we aren't in Crimea. It's even in our name."

"Everyone has to have a place where they belong." Mama reached out to touch Lutfi's shoulder.

"You know you belong here with us, don't you, Lutfi?" She sounded almost pleading, and Safi looked at her in surprise.

"We people without a homeland can only live in our memories," Grandpa said. "The Crimean Tatars remember, and it keeps us alive. If you were to look inside my head, you would find, oh, rifts wrought of grief; scars seared by the things I have seen and the things I have heard."

"And the Russians?" Ibrahim mused. "My grandparents told me that when they were deported, they asked their Russian neighbours, 'Why are they sending us away?' And the answer was: 'Only Comrade Stalin knows why.' Stalin's orders, and he could be harsh enough to his own people too. But what about the soldiers and officers carrying out those orders? All my studying can't help me understand what was in those Russians' heads."

"Not Russians," Grandpa corrected. "Soviets. Let me tell you about one Soviet: First Deputy People's Commissar for State Security Bogdan Kobulov."

Grandpa's voice took on a strange, mechanical precision, as though he were reading from an invisible textbook. Safi suddenly had the odd thought that this was not like Grandpa telling a story. It was almost as though the story was telling him.

"At eight o'clock on the evening of 19 July 1944, inside Bogdan Kobulov's head you would find … satisfaction. He and his colleagues have carried out an unbelievably complicated job, involving twenty-three thousand soldiers, a hundred jeeps, two hundred and fifty trucks, sixty-seven trains and a hundred and eighty-three thousand Crimean Tatars. The result: an entire nation removed quietly and without fuss. What remains of it after the long journey east and south is now settled in work camps, a useful source of slave labour.

"Kobulov is brushing his hair in the mirror and thinking of his telegram to Beria, head of the NKVD, informing him of successful project completion. He is annoyed to be interrupted by a message, but when he reads it his satisfaction evaporates rapidly. The message informs him that a number of small Tatar villages have been overlooked in the removal process, because of their remote location on a sandy strip along the east Crimean coast known as the Arabat Spit.

"Kobulov's reply is to the point. 'Get rid of those Tatars within two hours, or heads will roll.' He checks his watch. It is one hour to the victory banquet when they will drink to a long-cherished Russian dream finally come true: a Crimea cleansed of Crimean Tatars. His face in the mirror is suddenly pale. Comrade Beria is not renowned for his tolerance of mistakes. Kobulov knows that if his order is not carried out, the first head to roll is likely to be his own.

"Nine o'clock. The long table is loaded with champagne and cognac, caviar, some bowls of early Crimean peaches. Kobulov is in his dress uniform, the buttons and stars polished and shining. There is a brand new medal on his chest, for his achievements in Crimea. The assembled officers are lifting their glasses for the toast when an aide comes in and whispers in his ear. Kobulov's pale face reddens, and the officer sitting beside him hears his curt reply: 'Twenty-four hours then. And no more!' For the rest of that celebratory evening, Kobulov seems strangely subdued.

"Twenty-four hours pass, and everyone notices what a foul mood People's Commissar Kobulov is in. What is in his head as the hours drag by? It's unlikely that he has much imagination. If he wonders at all exactly how his orders are being carried out, it is only in terms of time and efficiency. The Arabat Spit has but one poor road and water on both sides; what would be best would be to load all the Tatars onto barges and move them out to the deepest part of the Azov Sea, then sink them. The Azov Sea is warm and shallow, popular among holidaying mothers and toddlers before the war. Still, with machine-gunners to mop up any swimmers, that should be effective enough.

"Nine o'clock again, and the message has arrived. Kobulov is with a few colleagues, and when he gets up with a full glass they frankly think he must be drunk. 'Comrades! To the achievement of our aims! For I can say without a shadow of doubt that *now* we have a Crimea without Crimean Tatars!'

"If you were to look inside Kobulov's head at this moment you would find ... relief. With luck, Comrade Beria will never find out about this little incident. No need to worry just yet about disappearing to Siberia or into an unmarked grave. Maybe he'll get to keep that medal after all."

Silence. There was nothing more in the unwritten textbook; no more story. There was just an old, weary man sitting by the fire with his family, and all of them were seeing how nearly fifty years ago and today and always out in the darkness the warm, shallow Azov Sea rolled and rolls over the loose tangled limbs, the staring eyes, the blood.

"Kobulov was shot," Ibrahim said quietly. "In 1953, when Stalin died, a secret Soviet court stripped him of his medals after all. Beria too; all those NKVD leaders were executed. That's in the records. But this story you tell us, about the Arabat Spit: I have never read of that in any records, and I don't suppose I ever will."

"Because they all died, those Crimean Tatars of the Arabat," Grandpa said. "There is no record and no one to remember them except us, who never saw what happened but who recall it as another wound, another scar that makes us what we are. Yes, inside my head my memories burn and burn, but I cannot be rid of them. Sometimes we have to burn for our people."

22

WHY DO THEY HATE US?

That morning the police disappeared. Their cars were gone, and when Lutfi went down to check, the hedge where they had sat was empty. The crowd of locals had gone too, leaving a mess of bottles and cigarette packets and torn-up notices. It was eerily quiet without them. Safi had almost forgotten the silence of Mangup-Kalye; now it came flooding back, undisturbed by the grumble of talk and insults, the hammer and tap of building. It didn't feel threatening any more. It felt peaceful and strange and a little bit sad.

"Perhaps they really did get bored and went away," Safi said hopefully.

No one else had time to speculate; they were too

tired and worried. Since the *Surgun* meeting several weeks ago the men had hardly slept, taking it in turns to keep watch all night as the locals grew more and more threatening. It was probably because of tiredness and not his usual scholarly abstraction that Ibrahim had slipped and fallen from the ladder as he fitted the gutter along the roof. The Tatar doctor who came out from Bakhchisaray said he had broken a rib. She had worked as a doctor in a city clinic in Uzbekistan, but here no one would give her a job.

Ibrahim lay in the *chaykhana*, his face pinched and thinner than ever. He needed to go to hospital, but without a residence permit and money, no hospital would accept him. The Tatars in Bakhchisaray had done their best. As well as the doctor, they had sent medicine and bandages. They would have sent money if they could. But no one had any to send.

The tooting of a horn broke the unaccustomed quiet. Safi thought she recognized it. She didn't dare run to investigate, in case the police hadn't really gone, but she watched from up the valley as the big blue and white bus came round the corner and slowed to a halt.

There was no Zarema; she had kept away from

them since the anniversary of the *Surgun*. Andrei got out and a few moments later he was looking hesitantly into the *chaykhana*.

"Zarema sent me. I've come to take your friend to hospital."

"They won't let him in," Mehmed snapped.

"I've got a friend who works in one of the Simferopol hospitals," Andrei explained. "They'll take him for free, apart from medications. I'm sorry, my bus is no ambulance, but if you help me carry him down there we can go right away."

"We can't pay," Papa said harshly. He was glaring at Andrei with what looked like fury.

Andrei flapped a hand, as though trying to wave the words away. "Doesn't matter. Later. Zarema asked me."

"She's got no business doing that. She'd be better looking to her own problems; we can take care of ours."

"I think she wanted to help." Andrei's voice was mild, but his face coloured.

Safi couldn't understand why no one was doing anything. Poor Ibrahim was lying looking like he wanted to die, and Papa and Andrei were wasting time glaring at each other.

Mama clearly felt the same. She took Ibrahim's hand. "Can you stand, or should we get a board for a stretcher? Help me, Mehmed."

By the time Mehmed and Refat had supported Ibrahim down to the bus he was white and gasping, and even Andrei looked concerned.

"We'll repay you as soon as we can," Papa said as the bus engine started up. "Keep track of the petrol cost, anything else, and we'll pay you back every penny."

Andrei leant out of the window. "You can repay me right now, by being a little kinder to Zarema," he said quietly. "She's told me what really happened with her husband. As I understand it, he left her. She's free to make whatever decisions she wants."

The bus drove away before Papa could answer.

Mama and Papa started arguing before they got to the house.

"We'll pay him back," Papa muttered feverishly. "Forty-five kilometres to Simferopol, that's about ten litres of petrol. And there's the damn hospital. We'll have to pay this friend of his."

"You heard him. He's doing it for free."

"I don't want Russian charity! I don't want his patronizing help or his traitorous kindness. Zarema's a fool. It didn't take her long to forget who she is; and now without Remzi she'll let Ismet grow up not knowing his roots, in a Russian household—"

"Remzi left her!" Mama shouted. Mama never shouted. "Your great heroic Tatar man left his wife and child, and Zarema stayed here because she knows this is where she belongs, and this is where Ismet belongs, and it's where Andrei and the Russians belong too. Can't you forget your stupid stiff-necked pride for just one minute?"

Safi exchanged appalled glances with Lutfi. Then they both turned and ran.

The tumbled tombs were hard to see in the shifting dapple of light and shade, as if they were not entirely there, ghosts themselves. It was cool and peaceful in the cemetery. Lutfi sat with his back to a tree root, angrily picking the moss from a grave. Safi looked at the path winding upwards. She'd never been to the plateau with Lutfi, not in all this time.

"Let's go up to the top."

"What for? It's just a load of old ruins."

"But it's wonderful up there."

She started to tell Lutfi about it. The flowers grew so thickly now, it was like brushing through a many-coloured curtain to get to some of the caves.

The pale stone radiated warmth and light; on it small lizards basked, darting away at the slightest sound, swift and dry as wind-blown leaves...

She realized he wasn't listening to a word she was saying. "Lutfi. Lutfi?"

Lutfi crumbled a handful of moss into pieces. "What?"

"What's the matter?"

He just kept breaking the moss into smaller and smaller pieces, until it was flakes of green and brown stuck to his fingers.

"Are you missing Larissa?" she asked him timidly. She hadn't dared mention Larissa since that argument they'd had weeks ago, about telling secrets.

"No," Lutfi said. "Why should I miss her? She's a bloody Russian, like all the rest."

Safi couldn't speak for a moment. Lutfi had spent all his time with Larissa. He'd been heartbroken at leaving her behind. He hadn't cared what nationality she was, neither had Larissa; they'd just been in love.

"I can't stand this!" she cried at last. "Why do they hate us so much? Why do you hate them? Back in Samarkand it never mattered. We were happy there; there was never this stupid arguing when we had a nice house and neighbours, Uzbeks and Russians and us—"

Her brother suddenly rounded on her in rage. "You know what you sound like, with your 'Uzbekistan was so wonderful; it was so nice; everyone loved us so much'? You sound just like Grandpa going on about this place. The roses, the sheep, the bloody tobacco field. And you know what? It's just as much rubbish. Uzbekistan was crap. It was never that great, and I bet Crimea wasn't either. And you know what really stinks? *That this is all we've got.*"

Lutfi jumped up and blundered away between the graves, not even following a path, just pushing straight into the bushes and trees as if he hated them. Safi stared after him. And then she turned and ran for the second time that day, as fast as she could up the steep path to the top of Mangup-Kalye.

From the tip of the plateau, the house in the valley was a tiny box. She couldn't see anyone around it, which was strange. But of course, Refat was in the bus taking Ibrahim to Simferopol, with Mehmed following in his car. Lutfi was off somewhere in the woods, and Mama and Papa were arguing. She wondered where Grandpa was. The whole valley was empty: no police, no locals down by the road, not even any visitors' cars.

In the worry of Ibrahim falling, no one had really noticed that the work he'd been doing, fixing up the gutter, was almost the last thing needed to finish the house. It was more modest than Papa had planned, but it had four walls, a roof and a chimney; it had a floor and a front door and windows. It stood alone and empty and unloved, this house that had taken all their money and effort, that had made the locals hate them, and nearly killed Ibrahim.

Safi knew she should be proud, looking at it. Instead she turned her back on it and wandered along to look out over the other side of the plateau. The road from Krasniy Mak was a violet ribbon skirting the edge of Mangup-Kalye. As she watched, a faint roaring reached her ears and a yellow vehicle came into view, moving slowly along the road. It looked like a bulldozer. Then came two cars, driving behind like a convoy. She watched idly for a moment, wondering where they were going.

But her cave drew her. The way to it was so familiar now, she could almost trace it with her eyes closed. There, inside the sunny solitary roundness of Safi's house, she wished she could stay for ever. She lay on the seat, her cheek to the warm stone, looking out at all of Crimea, from the mountains to the sea, laid below her like a gift. Grandpa called Crimea this almost-island, this green diamond, and said it belonged to her. It had belonged to her before she was born, but she didn't want it. All she wanted was this cave.

A few visitors were ambling around at the top of Mangup. Some of them had looked oddly at Safi, and one woman had asked if she was alone and if she was all right. Someone had even been in this cave not long ago. There was an apple core and a greasy scrap of paper on the floor, and a candle stub in one of the alcoves. Safi tossed the core out into the valley far below, and crossly put the paper in her pocket to throw away later. She hated to think of anyone else being here. This was the only place in the whole wide world where she felt at home, and she didn't see why she should share it with anyone.

She could still hear the roaring from the road below. It was getting louder. In fact, she thought she could hear shouting as well. It was odd that they were driving this way; there was nothing much along the road after their valley until you got to Bakhchisaray.

And then suddenly Safi knew, as surely as she

had ever known anything, where they were going. With a shriek she leapt up from the seat, pulled herself up out of the entrance of her house, and ran.

"Papa! Mama!"

She never knew how she got down the path. It was a blur of green and dark and treacherous stones and panic that she would be too late.

"Lutfi, come quickly!"

But no one came except the bulldozer. There were about five men hanging out the sides of the cab, shouting drunkenly. Behind, the cars came to a halt and more men got out. Safi recognized many of them from the crowd that had gathered by the pond. Laughing, they walked over to the two tents and with boots and sticks began smashing them to the ground.

"Stop!" Safi screamed from the edge of the woods. "Papa! Grandpa!" Her voice was lost in the cheer that went up from the bulldozer's cab. "Help! Police!" Then she remembered, the police had disappeared that morning.

Three men went up to Mama's *chaykhana* and casually leant against it. They leant and leant. The *chaykhana* creaked. One of the posts holding it up gave way with a sharp crack.

The bulldozer came on towards the house. The men whooped and yelled over its grinding roar.

"Papa!" Safi shrieked. She ran from the woods and out in front of the bulldozer, waving her arms. They wouldn't run her over; they would have to stop. "Stop, oh please stop! Go away!"

The bulldozer came on. The men driving it were drunk and wild; too late, she realized they probably hadn't even seen her. The blade of the bulldozer was right upon her. They weren't going to stop.

Safi screamed and closed her eyes. And then there were arms around her and she was snatched off her feet and the bulldozer had not touched her. She looked up and it was Papa, his face whiter and more terrible than she'd ever seen it. His arms round her were shaking. He was saying something, or perhaps he was shouting, but she couldn't hear because of the roar of the bulldozer and the splintering crash as it drove into their house. The walls cracked and split. The roof sagged.

For a moment, it was a struggle between the bulldozer and the house. Then the bulldozer won, and in a crumble of stone and cement the house collapsed.

23

WHERE IS LUTFI?

It felt like days later but it was that evening, when it was getting too dark to pick any more through the rubble, that a car engine broke the silence. At first they thought it was the drunk locals come back; then they hoped it was Mehmed returning from Simferopol. But Lena's fat, freckled father got out of the car. He gazed in embarrassed silence at the ruins of their house.

"Thought you might want a lift," he said at last. "My wife's made hot sweet tea. For the shock."

"Will you take us to Bakhchisaray, to our people?" Grandpa ground out.

"If that's what you want." Lena's father chewed his nail nervously. "But Krasniy Mak's nearer. For the little girl. My Lena's very worried about her."

"We have to go to Bakhchisaray." Papa couldn't bring himself to even look at Lena's father. "To get help. To search for Lutfi."

"Search for—"

"You destroyed our house," Papa shouted. "You nearly killed my daughter. Do you hear? You nearly killed her. And now my son is missing, and you want to give us hot sweet tea."

"I'm really very sorry." Lena's father took a deep breath. He was finding it hard to look them in the eye as well, but he managed. "Tell me what I can do to help, and I'll do it."

He took Safi and Grandpa to Bakhchisaray. Papa wanted Mama to go too, but she refused to let him stay alone in the valley. Safi clung to her parents. She was afraid to leave them in case they weren't there when she came back. In the end Papa had to pick her up and actually put her in the car next to Grandpa. "We'll be here. Remember, we never give up."

But Safi couldn't see how they could not give up now. She stared at Lena's father's face in the driver's mirror, and caught his abashed, curious eyes looking back.

"Did you know about today, what they were going to do?" she asked. "Did Lena know?"

His shoulders drooped. "Lena didn't know. She's worried to death about you. Listen, er, Ismailaga…" He stumbled over Grandpa's name. "I admit, I didn't agree with you Tatars coming back. Life in Crimea is hard enough as it is since the end of the Soviet Union: no wages, no jobs, water shortages. But I don't support what happened today. It's criminal, hooliganism, and I've told the chairman of the Krasniy Mak council so."

Grandpa said nothing. His big hand stroked Safi's head soothingly.

At the Bakhchisaray camp the Crimean Tatars met them with more than sweet tea. Within half an hour of their arrival they had mobilized. Those with cars took a big group to Mangup to guard what was left of the house and look for Lutfi. Others went to the squatters' camps and towns around Crimea to spread the news of what had happened, bringing reinforcements and warning them to be ready for trouble. The Tatars were angry. They took with them sticks and hammers and spades: everything they used for building that could also be used as a weapon.

They left Grandpa and Safi in a tent with a woman she did not know, but a little later the tent flap opened and Zarema appeared. "I came as soon as I could. Safi, *balam*, praise Allah you're all right."

"But Lutfi's gone. And the house, and everything." Safi leant against Zarema and felt the tears trickle down her face.

"Have you any idea where your brother might be, love?"

"I don't know! He went off into the forest on Mangup, and he didn't come back. Maybe he got lost, or the locals found him, or he just ... he just..." Safi couldn't finish the sentence. That he had just gone away.

"He'll be all right, a big clever boy like Lutfi. Don't worry." Zarema rocked her gently. "I've come from the hospital. Ibrahim's fine; he's much better."

"Does he know what's happened to his gutter?"

"Oh, Safi..."

"It was all for nothing. All that building and cooking and that horrible stove and it being like the Siege of Leningrad. It was a complete waste."

"Well, at least you've got rid of the stove."

"Don't try and cheer me up!" Safi shouted. "It's

all over, and I'm tired of it. I want to go home!"

But what did she mean by home? Their house in Samarkand had been sold now, and someone else was living there. Most of the Crimean Tatars, Mama and Papa's friends like Zarema, had gone from Uzbekistan, and the rest talked only of leaving. Home was in the box where the coffee pot and grinder lay swaddled in wool and silk, and now it was buried beneath a pile of rubble.

"Safinar." Grandpa was unpacking the bundle of things they'd salvaged from the wreckage of the house. It was pathetically small. He took from it a roll of faded cloth. "Safi. It's never all over, and we carry our homes with us. Come and look."

He unrolled the cloth, setting aside a tangle of old metal that had been wrapped in it, and spread out the scarf that was tucked inside. It was embroidered with dull gold thread in a stylized, curling pattern of leaves and fruit.

"It's a *marama*," Zarema said, leaning over to look. "A girl's headscarf. And I think it's wrapped inside this other cloth because it's a betrothal gift. Is that right?" She looked at Grandpa, but he did not reply. "It's old. People have forgotten these symbols now, how to embroider them and what they mean."

"Here is the *nar*, with the sweet seeds inside." Grandpa took Safi's unwilling hand and guided it to touch the round-bellied pomegranate design with its chequered heart. "The *nar* is a talisman of the family. Everyone has a family, and the *nar* is the pod enclosing the seeds, the people in the family, in health and harmony. See how it's divided into squares, to show that the family flourishes."

The gold thread was tarnished and scratchy. Safi picked at the embroidery, only half listening.

"And this is like life. The *nar* grows, and it divides. From each *nar* come stems, and from each stem falls a little drop, another life, a child. The child grows up, and the bud or flower grows a leaf. Safinar, listen."

"But it's not true." The threads were starting to unravel beneath her rebellious fingers. "None of it's true, and I'm tired of listening to stories! We're not all living nice and neat in little squares inside this *nar* thing. We're here and Lenara's in Uzbekistan and Lutfi's gone and—"

And I'm going, she realized she wanted to say. She was thinking of Lutfi's unrecognizable, angry face as he ran away into the trees on Mangup-Kalye. She was thinking of the clean, unburdened caves waiting

241

in the mountain. There was only her cave, empty and free of stories and history and hate, all that weight of misery and pride that the Tatars seemed to drag around with them wherever they went. There was only Safi's house.

"You kept telling us we were coming home, but this isn't home!" she cried. "It isn't where we belong and you've spoilt our family by bringing us back."

"*Safinar!*" Zarema said.

Safi couldn't look at her, or at Grandpa to whom she was never disrespectful, who she knew loved her the best. She jumped up and stormed out of the tent – and bumped into Refat and Mehmed.

"Have you found Lutfi?"

But she could see right away from their faces that they hadn't.

Not that day, nor the next. At Adym-Chokrak the Tatars were camped out behind a forest of new notices, but the locals did not come back. The streets of Krasniy Mak were empty. The bulldozer was back at the collective farm; the two cars and the drunken men seemed to have disappeared. The police were doing nothing.

Ravens soared high above the valley, turning

and flapping in the hot bright sky. The rocks on Mangup-Kalye baked. The rubble of the house had already been partly cleared and Mama's *chaykhana* propped back up, although it now leant at a slightly drunken angle. The valley simmered with angry, confident expectancy. The whole of Crimea simmered.

A low grumbling rose into the air, like the sound of the heat rising. It wasn't a bulldozer; it was a black Volga car with an official number plate, approaching very slowly, a police car behind it.

Safi crept her hand into Mehmed's, who was nearest to her. The cars halted a little way away from the pond. From the black Volga emerged, first, Lena's father, looking hot and flustered, then a man in a shirt and tie and a very smartly dressed woman holding a piece of paper.

"It's the chairman of the Krasniy Mak council," Refat said. "What's all this about?"

"Come to apologize for the inconvenience, I expect. *She's* the secretary from the Bakhchisaray administration. I'd know her anywhere; she's shut the door in my face enough times, the stuck-up tarty b—"

"Mehmed!"

"Sorry." Mehmed spat on the ground with vicious disgust.

"There's the little girl," Lena's father said to the chairman. To her alarm, Safi realized he was pointing at her. "They nearly killed her with that bulldozer. She jumped right in front of it."

"She looks all right to me," said the woman in a tone that said clearly, *Pity really.*

Refat took a threatening step forward. "What do you want? Come to pay Safinar compensation for what happened, have you?"

The woman's mouth curled in a sneer. "What right do you think you've got to demand compensation? I'm surprised you even know what the word means."

"We can't pay compensation," the chairman interrupted with a faint cough. "Your building was illegal. Those men were drunk from what we know, but we've been unable to track them down —"

"Unable to track them down!" Mehmed hooted with bitter mirth. "I suppose you can't explain either how they came to take away the farm bulldozer and then return it again all with no one noticing?"

"Hrrrm." The chairman cleared his throat. "Well now. We're all civilized people; no one wants children to get hurt —"

"*Some* of us are civilized," the secretary said, staring the Tatars down with her hard blue eyes.

"Tamara Vasilievna! Can I have the order, if it's not too much trouble?"

"Oh, if you must." With a look of shrivelling disdain, she gave the chairman the paper and sat back in the car.

"Asim Ismailov, Mehmed and Ibrahim Abdulaev, Refat Mamutov." The man looked in the crowd for Papa. "This order's from the Bakhchisaray administration. We had an emergency meeting after this, hrrrm, unfortunate incident. Your application for land has been reviewed, and in light of … of recent events the decision—"

Toot toot! To-o-o-t! *To-o-o-ot!*

"The decision has been made—"

T-o-o-o-ot! It was the familiar horn of the blue and white bus, but now it was blaring urgently. The bus flew round the corner and squealed to a halt. Andrei stuck his head out of the window.

"Quickly! Asim, where's Asim? The police have Lutfi."

"*What?*" Papa ran right past Lena's father and the chairman. "Where?"

"The same thing's happened at another squatters'

settlement. A fight started; the boys were throwing petrol bombs. The special forces turned up and they took a whole group of Tatars away. Lutfi was one of them."

A growl went up from the crowd. Mehmed was already running for his car.

"Where was it? How do you know?" Papa had actually reached up to grab Andrei's shirt and was dragging him half out of the window.

"Saw it," Andrei said. "In Molodezhnoe, Zarema's village."

It was only now that Papa seemed to notice that Andrei had blood on his shirt, and one eye was closing up in a red-black bruise.

"Couldn't stop them," Andrei said. "Came as soon as I could. Others are on their way to Simferopol. Get in."

Papa had already let him go and was turning to the others. "Molodezhnoe. Four of you in the back of the car."

"No," Andrei said. "There's nothing there, the fight's over. All of you, get in. I'll take you to Simferopol."

Papa paid no heed. The Tatars were dividing themselves between cars, their rage rising in a seething roar. The police were leaning out of their car windows, the village council chairman was hovering near his own Volga, holding his piece of paper indecisively. Through the shouting Safi heard him say plaintively, "Oh dear. Oh God. I thought you'd want to know that the decision is in your favour..."

"Where did they take Lutfi and the others?" Mama asked Andrei.

"We don't know."

Mama took Safi's arm and pushed her up into the bus. "All of you. On the bus."

"Elmira—"

"We're going to Simferopol." Mama's voice was quiet, but it cut like a knife. "All of us. We're going to demand Lutfi and the others' return, and we don't leave until we have them back."

24

ALL CRIMEA IS TALKING ABOUT YOU

Safi swayed on her feet, and felt Papa's hand quickly tighten to hold her up. She was squeezed between Papa and Refat, Mama and Grandpa and Mehmed around her all linking arms, part of a great human chain. Refat yawned hugely, and then clapped his hand over his mouth, looking embarrassed. It could have been the most amazing bravado, or else it was somehow disrespectful to yawn when the whole of Simferopol had been barricaded like a city under siege; when facing the Crimean Tatars were lines of riot police behind shields, and soldiers with guns that might start firing at any time. And still no one knew what had happened to the twenty-four Tatars from

Molodezhnoe, Lutfi among them, or when they would be freed.

Safi had told Lena that the Crimean Tatar movement was peaceful. But this felt like the beginning of a war. Anyone coming to join the cordon had to pass rows of closed-off side streets jammed with armoured troop carriers and blue and white striped buses like Andrei's, except these buses were full of soldiers and police special forces in black uniforms and men in no uniform at all. The Tatars who made it through the police lines talked about the ones who hadn't, who had been sent back or who had been beaten. But those who had been beaten got up and carried on; the ones who had been sent back just turned right round and came to join the cordon anyway. It stretched, sometimes fifty people thick, completely round the parliament building and down the street to surround the Cabinet of Ministers. No minister or deputy could get in or out without breaking the line, and the line would only be broken if the soldiers opened fire, or when the Tatars got what they wanted. They had promised that.

"Sorry," Refat muttered, smothering another yawn.

A moment later, Mehmed yawned too. Safi felt

her jaw muscles tingle and turned her face into Papa's arm as yawny tears came to her eyes. They had been there all afternoon, all night, all morning, and now it was nearing evening again. Somewhere the Crimean Tatar leaders were negotiating with the authorities, but on the street no one came to listen to them. There were only the crowds beyond the police lines yelling insults and the armoured vans that drove slowly up and down, shouting orders through loudspeakers: "Go home, Tatars. Your action is illegal and will be broken up…"

Startled, Ismet let out a sudden wail and a sleepy "Mama!" Andrei jogged him tiredly, and handed him to Zarema. Andrei had stood with them all night, since the police realized that he was using his bus to bring Tatars to Simferopol. Then they'd taken the bus away, and Safi supposed it was parked down one of those side streets now with all the other buses that had brought the soldiers and the crowds to throw stones and bottles at them.

"They aren't from Crimea," Andrei said, frowning at the businesslike hatred of the crowd beyond the police line. "I don't know where they're from. They've been brought here specially."

There were two other Russians standing with

Andrei, a middle-aged couple who had approached them nervously that morning. They'd stopped near Safi, perhaps encouraged to see children.

"Our son was arrested by the police too," the woman said. Her mouth quivered. "Three weeks ago. We still don't know where he is. They don't only happen to Tatars, these terrible, lawless things. We want to join you because you're stronger than us, but what you're demanding is right for everyone."

Safi looked up at Papa. His face was stony. Zarema was nodding.

"Of course you can join us," Safi said in a small voice, when no one else replied. Now the couple stood behind her, the woman smiling tentatively at Ismet.

A broken vodka bottle whistled over their heads and clattered to the ground beside Mama. The loudspeakers blared: "I repeat, you are breaking the law. Disband peacefully, or we will take action. This is an order."

There was no face to talk to, no one to argue with. The armoured van, the rows of blank riot shields on one side and the sealed parliament windows on the other were like the bulldozer, a blade that moved in to crush them without even seeing them. Safi's knees began to tremble. There was no one to rush in and save her this time, because Papa was squashed here next to her, with her family and the people she loved; they were all in the way of the bulldozer blade.

There was the sudden sharp tinkle of breaking glass, and Papa said, "Elmira!"

"How long must we stand here? I want my son back." Mama's eyes were burning. "All of them back, safe and unharmed." There were red spots in her pale cheeks, and on her fingers where she had cut them when she picked up the bottle and threw it through the parliament window.

"Right," said Refat. Loosing an arm, he removed his shoe and hurled it through the next window of the building.

"Whatever it takes," Papa said over the shower of breaking glass. He was looking at Mama with astonishment and recognition and fearful love. "Let's get these kerbstones up."

Refat's shoe came flying back out of the window, followed by a hole punch and a brass paperweight in the shape of a submarine.

"Who asked you here?" someone screeched

piercingly from inside. "What right have you? You deserve what you get, vandals!"

And then the missiles began to fly and the voice was drowned out by the windows shattering one by one by one, right the way across the parliament facade. The shards glittered beautiful as silver fish in the sunlight, and the noise of their falling, the angry crowd and the soldiers lifting their shields and guns was like the roar of the sea in Safi's ears. She didn't want to die. There were a number of things she wanted to do first, like find out if Crimean bus drivers and perhaps handsome heroes would start chasing after her when she was fifteen, and get Ibrahim to teach her some of that lovely Arabic lettering so she could write secret messages to Rustem on her school books, and go out dancing until after midnight in the kind of dress Mama said she couldn't wear till she'd finished tenth class. She wanted to meet Refat's outrageously grumpy mother when she came to Crimea and was rude about everyone, and show Lenara the caves on Mangup-Kalye, and go swimming with Lutfi and Lena in the sun-warmed, glassy salt sea.

"Don't shoot! Don't shoot! Oh, this is so scary..."

The noise of the sea broke up into separate sounds: shouting and clattering and, somewhere further down the line, shrill screams. Safi blinked. Scrambling towards her, hands up in the air, was Lena.

Safi's hand was curled round a chunk of concrete. She wasn't even sure how it had got there. Lena reached her and clutched her shoulders, panting. "Oh, wow, is this a riot?"

"What are you doing? How did you know we were here?"

Lena managed a magnificent snort. "Don't you realize, the whole of Crimea's talking about you?"

"If they're saying we started a riot, we didn't; we just want Lutfi back—"

"Silly, I don't mean about you the Tatars, though they're talking about that too. I mean the whole of Crimea's talking about *you*, Safi."

Something hit the back of Safi's head. It didn't hit very hard, but it was enough to mess up her careful plaits. Slowly she put her hand up to her head.

"After you jumped in front of that bulldozer and they thought they'd killed you..."

"They didn't even see me." There was something

wet and sticky matted into her hair at the back.

"They were totally drunk, but they saw you all right; and when everyone in the council heard about what happened, they changed their minds..."

Safi brought her hand down from her head and looked at it. There was red stuff all over her fingers. She felt suddenly hot and sick all over; she thought it was a great flush of embarrassment at what a stupid thing she'd done, one girl jumping in front of a bulldozer; it was like all these unarmed Tatars standing in front of half the army and smashing windows: stupid...

A warm wet worm crawled down the back of her neck. Screams dinned in her ears. A man was running along the line, waving his arms wildly and ducking the police truncheons. "Stop! They've agreed; they're bringing them back! All of them – we've got them back!"

"Safi?" said Lena. "You're not listening. Safi, you did it! Safi..."

Lena's face swung upside down and turned a strange shade of yellowish grey. There was a long torpedo-shaped object in front of Safi. She screwed up her eyes to see it better. It was a submarine, with curly lettering along its side that read ... that read

A Sausage, no, *A Souvenir from Crimea*. She tried to put out her hand to pick it up, and darkness shut down on her like a lid.

"Why does it say *sausage*, I mean *souvenir*? It isn't a souvenir; it's a submarine."

"What? Safi! Hey, Safi…"

She opened her eyes. Lutfi was leaning over her.

"Hello," she said. Her voice came out a strange croak.

Lutfi smiled lopsidedly. "Hey." His voice croaked too. "What are you babbling on about, nutty little sister?"

"Nutty brother. You look horrible." Lutfi's smile was lopsided because his lip was twice the size it ought to be, and half his face was covered in bruises.

"Speak for yourself. You should have seen you, with half a window stuck in your head – you looked like a robot from Mars."

Safi put up an experimental hand, and felt tightly wound bandages.

"Now you just look like an Egyptian mummy."

Giggling made her head hurt. "What happened? Is the riot over?"

"It was a demonstration, not a riot. Half of Simferopol's still blocked off but they've set up an emergency commission to deal with Crimean Tatar demands— "

"Have I been arrested too? Or have they let you out?"

"We've all been arrested. Yeah, this is it, Safi." Lutfi leant back, so she could see she was lying in bed in a dim room painted green. Mama and Papa were sitting squashed together on a chair near by. Papa had his arms round Mama and they looked very uncomfortable, but they were both fast asleep.

"Everyone? Grandpa, and Refat and Mehmed, Andrei and everyone?"

"Everyone."

Safi gazed round the drab little room. It looked oddly like a hospital. Was this prison, and would she stay in it for ever? Or would they finally all be sent back to Uzbekistan, and was this room the last thing she'd see of Crimea?

"It's not fair," she said in that unrecognizable, croaky voice. "We did everything – *everything* – so we could stay in Crimea. I don't want to go back!" She sat up and swung her legs off the side of the bed. Bright shapes danced in front of her eyes.

"Hey, lie down!" Lutfi sounded alarmed. "You can't get up yet. I was only —"

"What? What?" Mama sat up so suddenly that her head banged into Papa's chin with an audible thud. Papa yelped, overbalanced, and fell off the edge of the chair.

"Safi!" Mama exclaimed, untangling herself from Papa. "Oh, Safi, love, how do you feel? Don't try to move! Where are you going?"

"Safi!" Lutfi hissed in an agonized whisper. "I was only —"

The door burst open and Grandpa hurried in, followed by Zarema and Lena. Lena? Safi put a hand to her bandaged head. Surely Lena hadn't been arrested...

"You're awake!" Lena squealed. "Safi, you heroine you, that bit of glass nearly sliced your head off —"

"I don't want to go back!" Safi howled. "I don't want to go to prison. I want to stay in Crimea!"

"Safi..."

"Whatever are you saying?"

"Shall I call the doctor?"

Grandpa sat on the bed beside her and eased her head gently against his shoulder. "Calm down,

Safinar." His big hand rubbed her back soothingly. "Calm down. Shh. *Bir zamanda bar eken, bir zamanda yok eken.*"

"*Safi!*" Lutfi positively screamed under his breath.

Safi peeked at him out of the corner of her eye. He was pink with shame under the bruising. Finally realizing, she reached out and punched him on his knee, which was the nearest bit she could reach.

"Lutfi, you ... you ... you *liar!*"

25

SAFI'S HOUSE

The top of Mangup-Kalye was like paradise. Up you went and up, among gravestones, past ruins and through darkness, braving the ghosts on the way that held you back, the difficulties and fears and unsolved questions. There was clean cold water to wash them away, before you came out at the top and everything was changed.

Grandpa stepped out from among the trees, and the air and light burst on him like a great white parachute opening. It was so bright; it was so the same as it always had been that it hurt. Here at the top of Mangup you could see for ever, and all was clear. He clutched his chest and leant over, fighting to catch his breath.

"What's the matter? Oh, for goodness' sake, don't you go collapsing. If it's not enough that my fool of a son dragged me up here to catch a glimpse of my old village..." Refat's mother put her arm round Grandpa and squeezed tightly. She had the same high cheekbones and round black eyes as Refat, but while her son was the size of a bear, she was tiny, the skin under her eyes and between her fingers transparent as tissue paper. "I'm certainly not going to carry you, old man, so pull yourself together."

"I'm going..." Grandpa murmured. "Going..."

"Where? You aren't going anywhere! You can go to the devil if you like!" She dragged him out willy-nilly onto the plateau, onto the back of the hand. That strange, high green country was like an island in itself, closer to the sky than to the rest of the earth falling away on all sides in translucent layers of violet and blue, the almost-island Crimea fading further, further, until it met the silver line that was the sea.

"So where's my village then?" Refat's mother shaded her eyes and peered out into the distance. "I don't believe my great lump of a son ever went there; he certainly never dug up our family treasure."

Grandpa momentarily forgot the pain in his chest. "Do you mean to say there really is treasure buried there?"

"Of course there is. Some candlesticks, and the silver belt my father gave my mother as a wedding present. We buried it back in 1941, before those scheming devils of Germans arrived, to be on the safe side."

"Six paces past the walnut tree," Grandpa murmured.

"Oh well, I expect it's long gone, like everything else." Refat's mother breathed in deeply. "Couldn't steal the air, though, could they? Fill your lungs with it! Don't tell me that air doesn't make you feel better, old man."

"I'm younger than you, Fatime *Tata*," said Grandpa with dignity.

"And I bet you haven't had four strokes like I have; after the last one they thought they might as well bury me in Uzbekistan, but I made sure Allah knew I wasn't going to die so easily, not before I'd seen the homeland again. However much it has changed."

"Mangup-Kalye hasn't changed," Grandpa said. "Everything else has altered, but Mangup lasts for ever. And to think I was afraid to come up here…"

Fatime patted his arm with shrewd kindness, and let him drift off into his thoughts. On Mangup-Kalye, things had been changing for so long that no one could remember what they were like before. Who could imagine that once there had been houses and wine cellars, churches and mosques and kenessas? A whole city, buried now peacefully under flowers.

"What happened here? Where did they all go?" Mama looked out at the fathomless sky, framed by flowers and pale stone. She ran her fingers over the cave wall, and a piece of rock flaked away into her hand. There were delicate silvery spirals in it, the stone ghosts of seashells or sea creatures. "Look, fossils! This must all have been underwater once. Why did we never come up here before, Asim? All that time in the valley, and I never knew. It's wonderful."

"I remember you called it a terrible mountain once," Papa teased. "When you wanted to stay in Bakhchisaray."

"Well, it blocked out all the sunlight then. It will again, in winter."

"But by then we'll have got the electricity lines extended out from Krasniy Mak, so it won't matter."

263

Mama raised an eyebrow. "By winter?"

"I think so. Now we've got permission, everything will go much faster. And Andrei's worked as a builder; he's already told me a few things we did wrong on the house the first time, and suggested where we can get cheaper materials."

Mama held up a hand to Papa. "Oh, so Andrei's helping us now, is he? Or rather, we're accepting his help—"

Papa took her hand and pulled her out of the cave, into his arms. "Now, Elmira. I hope you aren't accusing me of being prejudiced against Russians. There are some very good ones out there, but it's still our country, not theirs."

Above them a red triangle hung high in the blue sky, soared downwards over the valley, did an impressive loop the loop and then returned to hang, trembling slightly in the wind. Ismet squealed with delight and Andrei could be heard instructing Zarema. "Look, you have to pull on the left string … that's right, not too far … no, not too much—"

The kite flew sideways and plummeted. Grandpa turned his head to watch it fall. "That's how we watched the aeroplanes, zooming along the valleys when there was a war being won and lost and we could see it all laid out below like a map, like a game that had nothing to do with us up here, because up here was paradise, where nothing was ever lost..."

"Watch out." Mehmed ducked. "Ibrahim!"

"Mmm." Ibrahim didn't take his nose out of his book. The kite missed his head by a fraction and Refat reached out and caught it before it tangled itself in a bush.

"One of these days..." said Mehmed, shaking his head. "You *were* reading a book when you fell off that ladder, weren't you?"

"Mmm?" Ibrahim gently blew a fat furred bumble-bee off the edge of the page, looking up after it as it flew away. "Where did that kite come from?"

"Exactly."

Ibrahim changed the subject. "So, Refat, when are you going to take your mother to Kermenchik?"

"I want her to see it from here." Refat waved out at the distant valleys and hills. "The whole village is probably waiting to jump on us if we go back, to make us show them where the treasure is. It's all Safi's fault."

"It wasn't me!" Safi had come over for the kite. "It was Grandpa!"

"Yes, but you know we can't be disrespectful to our elders."

"Oh, all right then. Sorry about the treasure, Refat."

"You're our treasure," said Refat. He leant back into the warm, thyme-scented grass and gazed upwards, heaving a contented sigh. "This is our treasure."

"And it's in our back garden," said Mehmed.

Ibrahim turned the sunlit page. "'Lord, build for me a home with Thee in the garden…'"

"'…and deliver me from the unjust people',"
Mehmed finished. "Speaking of which…"

It looked like everyone had chosen to come to Mangup-Kalye this summer Sunday. Strolling along the plateau came a Russian family: the chairman of the Krasniy Mak council with his wife and two children.

The chairman glanced at them quickly and then away. Then he looked back, clearing his throat. "Good afternoon."

"Afternoon."

"*Salaam aleikhum.*"

"Lovely day," said the chairman's wife, nodding coolly at Safi. "How are you feeling?"

"Fine." Safi blushed. The bandage had come off a week ago, leaving a small sprouting patch of hair that fortunately was mostly hidden under her plaits. It wasn't fair: Lutfi had come out of all this with a bandaged wrist and bruises that made him look interesting and heroic, and she had to have this silly fuzzy bit where they'd shaved her head to put in stitches.

The family walked on quickly, almost bumping into Lena as she popped out of a hidden cave entrance. She looked disappointed.

"I thought it was Lutfi. We were playing hide-and-seek with my little cousin, and I guess he got bored since he never came to find us—"

"Gotcha!" Lutfi jumped out from behind a bush and grabbed Lena one-handed. Shrieking, she tore herself away and dashed off along the plateau.

"She's hard work, that girl." Lutfi sat down next to Safi. "Look at that view. Just look…" His voice tailed away and he went quiet, gazing.

"You've never been up to the top of Mangup before, have you?" Safi scrunched the plants under her hand, and the clean scent of them was suddenly dizzying. "Isn't it fantastic?"

"I've been up on the other side," Lutfi said. He pointed out over their valley to where the lower cliffs rose. "That's where I was when they knocked the house down."

Safi looked at him sideways. Lutfi was concentrating on picking up the tiny green-gold crab apples, no bigger than acorns, that scattered the grass.

"There was nothing I could do. I never saw you."

"Oh, well..." Safi blushed again. "I didn't do much."

"That's not what everyone else thinks."

"Anyway, the next house we build will be much better, now we've got rights to the land," Safi said encouragingly.

"And everything's going to be all right, *inshallah*." Lutfi had that light that wasn't sunlight in his green eyes. "You haven't heard the news, I suppose. Lots of the Tatars are talking about it. The Chechen Republic has split, and the Russians are saying they'll go to war with Chechnya."

"To war?" The Chechens had been deported at the same time as the Tatars, but they had been permitted to return home years ago. Safi had heard rumours that Chechnya, now part of Russia, wanted independence, but she hadn't paid much attention.

"You see. You think just because we get to build our house, everything's all right. The Chechens are Muslims like us from the former Soviet Union, and the Russians are going to war with them just like one day they'll be at war with us."

Safi sat quiet. The sun poured into their skin, their bones; it was like sitting under a great healing hand. Lutfi knew what she wanted to say: they had Crimea, they had Mangup-Kalye, this garden with God, and it was their home, and wasn't that enough to think about for now?

After a moment, he put an arm round her, breathing in deeply the flowers and the air and the huge sunlit space. "Yeah, it is fantastic. Nutty sister."

"Hey, lazybones!" Lena peeked out from a tangle of branches close by. She waved and then ducked back, giggling.

"You're not really playing hide-and-seek. How old are you?"

"Oh, she just wants to get me into the bushes." Lutfi stuffed a handful of miniature apples down the back of Safi's dress. She was so surprised she screamed in true Lena-style.

"Hey!" A hail of the tiny golden apples came flying out of the thicket, bouncing around their heads.

Safi suddenly couldn't stop laughing.

"I'm coming to get you!" Lutfi dived in, roaring. The bushes shook violently, and muffled shrieks came out of them. More crab apples rolled down the slope towards Safi. She waited, but Lutfi didn't come out again.

She wasn't sure she minded. Mehmed and Ibrahim and Refat were still sitting with their legs dangling over the edge of the plateau, contentedly annoying one another. Papa and Mama were perched on a ridge of broken wall overgrown with pink and yellow flowers. Mama's head was on Papa's shoulder. Soppy parents. Zarema was flying the kite with Ismet and Lena's younger cousins; Refat's mother was talking energetically to Andrei about something, no doubt being rude, and he was listening and laughing...

Quietly Safi turned away and began to step over the springy, flowery grass, past all the visitors enjoying the perfect summer day, the caves echoing with cheerful voices. She wanted to be alone for a while.

The sun had gone from her cave, but left its sweet warmth behind. The candle was on the shelf, and there was a slightly wilted bunch of flowers lying on the windowsill. Safi sat, letting the curve of the bench hold her comfortably, as it must have held all those hundreds of other people who had passed through leaving scarcely a trace: a smoothed edge of an alcove, a hollow in the stone, a handful of flowers, an apple core.

There were slow, fumbling footsteps outside the window, where as far as she knew there was only a hundred-metre drop. A big hand reached round the edge of the window, an arm, and then her whole grandfather followed. He stepped carefully over the sill and stood in her cave.

"How did you get here?" Safi leant out of the window. There was a narrow ledge she'd never noticed, and a very steep, worn flight of steps curving up the outside of the cliff. "I thought there was only one way in."

"Through the hole in the ceiling? I was always too big for it." Grandpa put his hand gently on the pillar. "Safi's house," he said.

"How did you know? Oh! Did you come here when you were young and living in Adym-Chokrak?" Safi felt slightly affronted. This was *her* cave. "You never told me any stories about it." She fell silent, looking at her grandfather's face. He ran his hands slowly and lightly over the roof, round the alcoves, the way you might touch something delicious – rose petals, the silken lip of a shell – to see what it felt like. "Why did you call it Safi's house, *Khartbaba*?"

"Because that's its name. Here on Mangup nothing changes; nothing is lost. Can you reach, Safi?"

"Reach what?" Safi knelt up on the seat. The alcoves, she only noticed now that Grandpa showed her, had faint traces of paint on the sides: sky blue, scarlet and tawny yellow, too faded to see what the patterns had once been. In the corner of one was a crack in the stone.

"In there. You've got small fingers, like hers."

"There might be spiders." But she was too curious to really care. She inched her fingers into the crack, and felt a cold, sharp edge. "There is something in here…"

Carefully she eased it out and it fell into her hand: a rusty black metal key, with sharp flanges and the end shaped like a heart.

"Is that what you were looking for?"

Grandpa felt around in his pocket, and dropped into Safi's hand a second key. It was slightly larger, but it was of the same dark metal, with the same heart-shaped handle.

"What do they open?"

"Safinar's father was a locksmith. He made both of them, the keys to our houses."

"Which houses? Who's Safinar?" It was funny talking about someone with the same name as herself. "Is this her house?" Safi sat back down on the seat, hugging her knees expectantly, warming the keys in her hand.

"Safinar lived in the village on the other side of Mangup-Kalye, near where Krasniy Mak is now. She used to bring the cow up here to pasture in summer, where the grass is sweetest."

"I've seen the cow," Safi said eagerly, but Grandpa went on as if he hadn't heard.

"She locked her house and came up here all day, with an apple and a piece of pie wrapped in a bit of paper. We'd meet in this cave. In Safi's house. From up here we watched the war going on, and tried to spit on the planes flying down the valleys. We sat on this bench and looked out at Crimea. We were going to be married, when the war was over and we were old enough."

Safi waited. It wasn't like one of Grandpa's usual stories.

"Then what happened?"

"We sat in this cave and we watched the soldiers come for us on a May morning in 1944. I was seventeen, and she made my world go round." Grandpa's face seemed to crack. "It was a long time ago."

"Did she go with you, into exile?"

"She didn't have to. She was only half Tatar; her mother was Russian. Safinar could stay."

"Maybe she's still here," Safi said gently. "You could try to find her. I'm sure she remembers you…"

"Here on Mangup nothing changes; nothing is lost. What a silly old fool I am, eh, Safi?" He put his hand on her head, smoothing her plaits. "Not much of a story, is it? It's time you made your own stories. Now I've got to get back up these steps for the last time."

"Be careful."

Anxious, she leant out to watch him stepping with surprising lightness up the worn staircase and up, up out of sight, into the blue.

EPILOGUE

*B*ir zamanda bar eken, bir zamanda yok eken.
*That means, "sometime it was, or sometime it wasn't at
all." It's the proper way to start a story, Grandpa told me.*

*He told me it's time I made my own stories, but he's left
me with an unfinished one. I'm still sitting in this cave, in
Safi's house that isn't really mine after all; it belongs to
another Safinar, and I don't think he told me the truth. Or
he let me think that the end was different. She went with
him into exile, I'm sure of it. How else would Grandpa
know her key was still here? Safinar went with him into
exile, even though she didn't have to, and she died on the
way. Grandpa didn't want to tell me that, because all his
stories are too sad, and if I'm going to make up my own,
I want them to be happier.*

But at the same time, you can't really lie about the past, can you? Or the future. I can't pretend that everything's going to be all right now. We got permission to rebuild Adym-Chokrak, but at Molodezhnoe they're still squatting the land, and at all those other Tatar villages. We Tatars still can't get jobs in Crimea, we can't even get treatment in hospital. There's going to be a war in Chechnya and maybe Lutfi will go away and fight it, or maybe he's right, one day there'll be a war here too. How many more bulldozers will we have to jump in front of before things come right, hey, Safinar? Safi's house! Listen! What happened here? What happened to all the people who lived here, and built houses and told stories? What's going to happen to us?

I know you're listening. You're still here, aren't you, Safinar? I met your cow. It was you who put the ivy over the path by the cemetery, who took my hand and led me onto Mangup-Kalye. You showed me your house. Maybe you went with Grandpa into the cattle trucks and died there; or maybe you went to, I don't know, Moscow, and studied to be a ... a brain surgeon and married one of your patients who fell in love with you on the operating table. Bir zamanda bar eken, bir zamanda yok eken. There, I've made up my first story.

But up here on Mangup-Kalye everything changes; nothing is lost. You're still here in Safi's house, looking after us.

Or maybe that bit of glass in my head really has made me go a bit nutty.

I look at the keys in my hand, their black iron warmed by my skin. They belong together. Kneeling up, I push them both carefully back into the alcove. That's the end of their story, to lie together hidden safe in the stone, until someone finds them and wonders what they are. But our story's just beginning.

I pull myself up again through the hole in the corner of the cave, up onto the plateau, onto the top of our world, our paradise. It's all golden up here now as the sun sinks down. You never saw so much gold, filling the valleys, gilding the hills; and the distant sea's shining brighter than stars. I run to where they're waiting for me, my family and all the others, in a row like the Crimean Tatar Star Alley, with a space at the head for Grandpa, and a space at the end where Lenara should be. I can't wait for her to come. I want to show her everything: Mangup-Kalye and our new house and school and the sea.

"Where have you been, love?" Mama gives me a slightly anxious kiss. She's all warm and soft from the sun. "You're all right, aren't you?"

"I'm fine. I've been exploring." I will show them Safi's house, but not yet, not quite yet.

"Isn't this Mangup-Kalye the most wonderful place?

Don't you think Lenara will love it?"

So Mama has been thinking about Lenara too.

"Of course she will," I say. "Let's build our new home as quick as we can so she can come over. How long will it take this time?"

Papa laughs at me. He's bright-eyed and fiercely happy. "Not long. After all, we've had some practice."

Notes and Acknowledgements

All the characters in this book, except Catherine the Great, Joseph Stalin, Soviet Security Chief Lavrenty Beria and First Deputy People's Commissar for State Security Bogdan Kobulov, are fictional. The things that happen to them, however, are closely based on real events.

The deportation of the Crimean Tatars from Crimea in 1944 is documented in telegrams sent to Stalin by Kobulov and his associates. There is no published official documentation concerning the fate of the Tatars from the Arabat Spit; the story in Chapter 21 is based on eyewitness accounts published in the Crimean Tatar newspaper *Yani Dunya*.

The verses in Chapter 1 are from *Tatarligim* by Shevki Bektore, and in Chapter 20 from Numan Chelebi Jihan's *Ant Etkenmen*, which has been adopted as the Crimean Tatar national anthem. Chelebi Jihan (1885–1918), poet, lawyer and nationalist, was the first head of the Crimean Tatar National Directorate, which governed Crimea for a few months between 1917 and 1918. He was arrested and shot by Bolshevik Black Sea Fleet sailors. Shevki Bektore (1888–1961) developed the first Crimean Tatar alphabet based on Arabic script; he was arrested in the 1930s for nationalist activities and spent years in Soviet prison camps before emigrating to Turkey in the 1950s.

Many other ethnic groups in the Soviet Union were deported from their homes to Siberia and Central Asia in 1944. However, all but the Crimean Tatars were allowed to return in the 1950s, after Stalin's death. Over a quarter of a million Crimean Tatars finally came back to Crimea between 1987 and 1995.

Sadly, Safi is right not to pretend that "everything's going to be all right now". The land disputes in Crimea continue to this day. Crimean Tatar religious and historical sites are being destroyed, and there are sometimes violent clashes between Tatars and Russian nationalist groups. However, Tatar classes and schools have been established, and Crimean Tatar culture is visibly reviving, an intrinsic part of the modern Crimean Autonomous Republic in Ukraine. Most importantly, there is no war.

In reality, the Crimean Tatar village of Adym-Chokrak has never been rebuilt. But on the other side of Mangup-Kalye the village of Haja-Sala has, and I have borrowed elements of its geography for this book. Similarly, Kermenchik has in fact been renamed Vysokoe (which means "high"), but another Tatar village, Ozenbash, really was given the new name Happy. I have also taken some liberties with the dates of some real events.

This book could not have been written without the generosity of the Crimean Tatars who invited me into their homes, fed me coffee and cakes and shared their astonishing stories. I am vastly grateful to all of them. Especial thanks to Lutfi and Ayshe Osmanov and family for unending kindness, patience and inspiration; Limara and Ayder Isayev, who recall their mother Shefike's stories as if they were their own and took me to see her house in Kermenchik; and Halide Kipchak and Nikolai Chernigovtsev for Crimean salt.

L.H.

Glossary

Italicized words are Crimean Tatar, Uzbek or Arabic words commonly used by Crimean Tatars

aga older brother, uncle: a term of respect
ana mother
balam little one
bogcha plain handkerchief for wrapping betrothal gifts from a suitor; also a larger cloth which a girl would embroider and use to wrap her trousseau
chaykhana tea house
chebureki fried meat pasties
churchkhela Georgian snack made of walnuts and raisins threaded on strings and dipped in honey and pomegranate juice, commonly sold in Uzbekistan
collectivization process in 1930s Soviet Union when private property was taken from its owners and turned over to state ownership in collective farms
Crimean Tatars a Turkic Muslim people who have lived in the Crimean peninsula, now part of Ukraine, for over seven centuries
inshallah God willing
kalpak traditional Crimean Tatar hat made of sheepskin
Karaims Turkic-speaking people who follow Karaite Judaism and have lived in Crimea for many centuries

kenessa   Karaim place of worship

khartbaba   grandfather

kobete   meat pie

Koran   Islam's holy book

lagman   soup with noodles, vegetables and meat

lyepushki   flat loaves of bread

marama   long white or cream headscarf traditionally worn by Crimean Tatar women

medresse   Islamic upper school

nar   pomegranate

NKVD   Soviet state security police, predecessor to the KGB

perestroika   process of restructurization that led to collapse of the Soviet Union in 1991

plov   dish of spiced rice, chickpeas and meat

Ramadan   month of fasting in the Islamic calendar, when it is forbidden to eat from dawn to sunset

Salaam aleikhum   Islamic greeting meaning "peace be upon you"

Stalin, Joseph   leader of the Soviet Union from the late 1920s until 1953

Surgun   exile

tamga   symbol like a pair of golden scales on the Crimean Tatar flag

tata   older sister, aunt: a term of respect

zelyonka   green-dyed iodine

Amnesty International

Safi and her family have returned to their homeland after being forcibly deported many years earlier. The prejudice and persecution that they face are sadly all too common for people who go back to their countries of origin after time in exile. Having a home and belonging to a country are fundamental human rights, but they are denied to many people around the world.

Human rights are basic principles that allow us the freedom to live dignified lives, free from abuse, fear and want, and free to express our own beliefs. Human rights belong to all of us, regardless of who we are or where we live.

Amnesty International is a movement of ordinary people from across the world standing up for humanity and human rights. Our purpose is to protect people wherever justice, fairness, freedom and truth are denied. We aspire to create a world in which we can all enjoy our basic human rights.

Youth Groups
In the UK we have an active membership of over 550 youth groups. Youth groups are gatherings of young people in schools, sixth form colleges or youth clubs who meet to campaign for Amnesty International. They hold publicity stunts, write letters to government leaders and officials, fundraise, get publicity in their local paper, hold assemblies and create displays. You can also join as an individual member and receive magazines and letter-writing actions.

If you would like to join Amnesty International, set up a youth group, or simply find out more, please telephone our Education and Student Team on 020 7033 1596 or email student@amnesty.org.uk

Amnesty International UK, The Human Rights Action Centre, 17–25 New Inn Yard, London EC2A 3EA. Tel: 020 7033 1500.

www.amnesty.org.uk

"It is difficult to explain how greatly our life changed after that first postcard. I never felt lonely any more... Every letter was a miracle – they changed my life, they gave me hope."

Marina Aidova, who was 8 years old when her father was arrested and imprisoned by the Soviet authorities. Amnesty International asked its members to write to Marina and her mother Lera.

"Amnesty's greetings cards really helped me in prison. In total, I received more than 4,000 – amazing! I read each one: the best, I think, were those from children and other student activists... It amazed me to see that those children know about human rights. What a good omen for the future!"

Ignatius Mahendra Kusuma Wardhana, an Indonesian student who was arrested at a peaceful demonstration in 2003 and spent more than two years behind bars, where he was beaten and threatened.